Call It What You Want.

ALISSA DEROGATIS

You'll always be my favorite almost.

If this story could be told through songs:

Prologue

SLOANE · DECEMBER 2018

The sun pours through the small window in my bedroom as I roll over and snooze the 6 a.m. alarm. Most New Yorkers are already wide awake, grabbing their oat milk lattes and gluten-free bagels, while my head is pounding from a bottle of wine and three hours of sleep. In an instant, the memory of last night's events floods back and I feel the agony coursing through my veins all over again.

The pain still lingers. I remember how much it hurt just to look at him. He had always been the one to make me feel safe, but last night was different. It was as though he'd taken a knife and repeatedly plunged it into my chest. Each time I looked at him, the wound was reopened, the pain as fresh and raw as the first time. It was like death by a thousand cuts.

"I can't do this anymore," he cuts me off mid-sentence. "I think this, us, needs to end."

I'm holding a glass full of my favorite Cabernet, and within seconds, it's out of my hand and on the floor. Almost as if it's instinct, I bend down to pick up the pieces. I hate messes and I'd rather focus on anything but this conversation right now. I look down at my hands to see that my right palm is gushing blood. Why can't I feel it? Why can't I feel anything? I watch as he pulls out his phone to call us an Uber. He's moving so quickly, but in my world, it's like time has stopped. I stare at him as he frantically moves around my kitchen, grabbing anything we might need for the emergency room, and I wonder where the guy I met in college went— the guy in the worn-out Yankees t-shirt with the soft smile and trusting eyes. I never thought I could hate him, and yet.

I can't even look at him. I never want to see him again, but at the same time, I don't want him to leave. Ever. I've loved him for over two years. How could he end two years with four words?

I can't do this.

The words are on replay in my head as if they're a new Taylor Swift song that I'm trying to memorize every line of. I think the worst part is realizing that somewhere, deep down, I knew it the entire time. I knew he wouldn't be able to get where I wanted him to. I just hoped that I was wrong.

No, we never dated. He's not an ex-boyfriend. He's an ex-almost. Maybe that's all we'd ever be— an incomplete sentence or a book that someone put down halfway through and never picked back up. Finished without an ending.

Part 1

THEN · 2016

Chapter 1

The first time I ever locked eyes with Ethan Brady was in a passing moment. It took me years to realize that life is just a succession of these so-called passing moments. If it's a painful moment, it will pass. If it's a perfect moment, it will also pass.

That particular moment occurred on one of the hottest days of the summer. Even with the coastal breeze, the heat in North Carolina was brutal. Unfortunately for me, it was also senior year move-in day, which meant carrying boxes up two flights of stairs for hours. Usually, one of my parents would be in tow, but my mom was called into work last minute and my dad wasn't always the most reliable. So, I had to do it all myself.

My mom was a pediatric surgeon. When I was growing up, she transferred hospitals every few years until she finally landed a position at Duke. My dad's career as a writer was flexible, so we were able to move wherever my mom needed us to. Quickly after publishing his first novel, my dad became a New York Times Best Selling

Author. Little did we know, that would be the first and last book he ever wrote. His agent dropped him after he missed his deadline four times. No matter how hard he tried, he just couldn't write. He started drinking a lot, mostly while my mom was at work. Eventually she had enough of it and asked him to move out.

When I was younger, I used to admire my parents' relationship. Things I used to consider "gross", I now realize were beautiful. Kisses in the car, holding hands in restaurants, cuddling on the couch. How can two people go from not being able to get enough of each other to never wanting to speak again? I'd never been in love, so I guess I wouldn't know.

The wood creaked under my feet as I started down the stairs for what would be my last trip from the car to my apartment. I noticed that the parking lot was now full of students with their parents— unloading cars, breaking down boxes and saying their goodbyes. I couldn't help but miss mine.

Ascent Student Living was no different than any other off-campus apartment complex. It was new and made up of eight buildings, all different shades of blues and greens. One of my favorite parts of living at the beach was that everything was prettier. The architecture of most buildings and shopping centers mimicked the aesthetic of a small beach town and even though we were a good twenty minutes from the ocean, the bright colors and palm trees made it feel closer. When I was applying to colleges, I was so excited to finally get to decide where I lived instead of following my mom up and down the east coast. The options were endless, but I decided to stay in North Carolina a little while longer. I settled on Wilmington

College where I'd major in English and minor in journalism. Then after I graduated, maybe I'd move to New York City and become a writer. A girl could dream.

After the weight of choosing a school was lifted, I finally started to enjoy what I had left of senior year—that's when I met Carter. Carter was the first crush I had since middle school. He had brown hair and these piercing hazel eyes that made me uneasy. Some of my friends said he looked like Christian Bale. I never told him I thought so because I didn't need to feed his ego any more than I already had.

Carter was, in ways, a breath of fresh air. He made me both excited and nervous at the same time. The nights I spent with him were adrenaline-pumping because I never knew what came next. He asked me to senior prom and showed up at my house with his mom and a corsage that didn't match my dress, but of course I wore it anyway. I lost my virginity that night. I thought it would be so much different. I was expecting this grand, romantic gesture and instead it was just a few minutes in a spare bedroom at my friend's house that resulted in a broken condom.

A few weeks later, my parents sat me down and told me they were getting a divorce. I was angry with them for ruining the summer before I went away to college. I had finally made it to my semi-adult life, and they were ripping the rug right out from under me at the time I needed stability the most. For the rest of the summer, I had sex with Carter whenever I could— while our parents were at work, in cars in parking lots, at parties, after parties— I was willing to do it whenever and wherever because I thought it would make him love me and I was desperate to not be alone.

3

Spoiler alert: sex never makes someone love you.

I spent the next year hoping we'd become more than a hook-up and the year after that trying to meet someone who compared to him. Fast forward to the middle of sophomore year when I decided to swear off dating until I graduated college— life got so much better when I stopped looking for love in every guy I met. I started to enjoy school, meet new friends and finally make peace with my parents' divorce.

I lifted the last box out of my car, closed the trunk and headed up the stairs to my second-floor apartment. Every few seconds I alternated looking down at my feet and then straight ahead to make sure I didn't miss a step and trip.

As I turned my gaze, my eyes landed on him, and I couldn't help but notice his impressive stature. He stood tall and upright, exuding confidence with his broad and muscular build. His dark brown hair was tucked neatly under a backward cap, accentuating his chiseled facial features. He wore a grey Yankees t-shirt, which seemed to have been washed and dried numerous times, but still clung to his form in a flattering way. The casual attire and relaxed demeanor only added to his allure, making him seem approachable yet intriguing.

"Need some help with that?" he asked.

"No, I'm okay."

I finally made eye contact with him. His brown eyes were familiar, like I'd looked into them before.

"That's me right there." I managed to stick my elbow out and point in the direction of the door that said 3221.

"See you around then, neighbor."

I didn't know his name, but I really wish I did. I wished I knew everything about him.

I walked inside of our apartment to my roommates, Lauren and Jordan, blasting music and laughing in the kitchen together. Before I joined them, I set the last box down in my bedroom. The rest of my unpacking could wait until tomorrow.

"Did you see all the hot guys in the parking lot? I'm so glad we got into Ascent. I heard so many people were waitlisted," Lauren said.

"Waitlisted for a college apartment complex?" Jordan asked. "That's insane. It's not Harvard."

I met Lauren Ellis and Jordan Coleman when we all got assigned the worst freshman dorm, Moore Hall. It was the only high rise on campus that hadn't been torn down and rebuilt yet. Lucky for us, we were among the last people to live there. I'd like to think the experience that was Moore Hell, as we called it, made us closer.

Lauren was a platinum blonde that never missed a hair appointment, even if it meant skipping class. She was strong-minded, always smiling and could land pretty much any guy she wanted. Jordan was the most free-spirited of us all and the most selfless person I'd ever met. She had a go-with-the-flow attitude that could convince me to do almost anything, and just by looking at her, you could tell she grew up at the beach. The three of us were so different yet fit together so perfectly.

Moving around so much when I was younger prevented me from forming long-lasting friendships. I found it easier to avoid getting emotionally invested in people that I knew I'd have to say goodbye to eventually. Lauren and Jordan provided me with a new perspective on friendship. They were a source of comfort and support during both the happy and trying times, and they made me realize I was missing out on such an important bond.

"I call dibs on the dirty blonde with the longboard!" Lauren laughed.

"You act like that's not a description of basically every guy on campus," Jordan replied.

"Just wait until you see who I'm talking about," Lauren opened the refrigerator and tossed us each a Twisted Tea. "Courtesy of my parents, our congratulatory move-in present was a fully-stocked bar."

"Can they just adopt me already?" I laughed, even though I wasn't joking. "Tell us more about the longboard guy."

"Okay, so you'll never believe this, but he was trying to get into our apartment this morning. He lives in the unit above us and for a solid ten minutes was banging on the door and yelling that his key fob wasn't working. When I finally opened it, he realized he got the unit numbers mixed up and was so embarrassed. He did ask for my number though and already texted me, so I'd call that a win."

"I hope his roommates are hot!" Jordan shouted from her room.

"What're you doing in there?" I replied. "It's pregame time; unpacking can wait."

"Well, our summer writing assignment can't."

"Shit."

I grabbed my Twisted Tea and headed to my room, shutting the door behind me. I looked around at the progress I made today; everything was pretty much in its place besides a few pieces of wall art I still needed to hang. I sat down at the cheap IKEA desk that Ascent provided each bedroom with, opened my laptop and pulled up the assignment. I chose English as my major because I'd always loved to write. Since I didn't grow up with siblings, I wrote fictional stories and kept journals to occupy myself.

I finished the assignment in record time and then made my way into the bathroom to get myself ready for our first night out as seniors. In the mirror, I stared at the girl looking back at me. She had medium-length auburn hair that had a naturally frizzy wave to it. You'd never know it though because she almost always curled it. She had hazel eyes and freckles that came out of hiding in the summer months. She had never been super confident in herself, but she was beautiful. She just hadn't heard that from anyone, besides her parents of course.

After I finished my makeup, I scanned the closet for an outfit to wear. I wanted to look good but not draw too much attention to myself. I settled on a pair of denim shorts, a white crop top with a lettuce hem and my go-to shoes— white Converse.

On Thursday, it was tradition that every student made their way over the bridge to Wrightsville's favorite sports bar— Jerry's. So, we took a few shots, piled into an Uber and made our way to kick off what I hoped would be an amazing senior year.

"Can I get you a drink?" are six words every 21-year-old wants to hear. I spun around and was face-to-face with the guy from the stairwell.

"Sure." I played it cool.

"Two Mich Ultras," he said, sliding the bartender cash.

"Bold of you to assume I'm a beer girl," I tried to flirt.

"Well, you're holding an empty bottle and it's dollar beer night, so it wasn't really much of a stretch." He laughed a little before chugging the rest of his beer and placed it on the sticky bar. I could feel my face go flush.

"I know, I was just testing you." I raised an eyebrow. "Observant, I like it."

"I was surprised to see you're drinking beer though; most girls still opt for a vodka cran even on dollar beer night."

"If I drink liquor, the night usually looks a lot different for me. I want to at least remember the first night of senior year, you know?"

"So, a senior huh? I would've guessed younger. What're you studying?"

"English and journalism. You?"

"I'm in the business program but I really want to get into sports broadcasting, so I considered journalism. I might pick up a minor this year if I can fit it in before graduation."

"Oh, you're a senior? I would've guessed younger." I threw his own joke back at him.

"Touché. Are you not into younger guys?" The corner of his mouth curled slightly into a smirk. It was at that moment I knew I was in trouble.

"Thanks for the drink." I smiled. "I better go find my friends though."

"Ethan Brady." He stuck out his hand. "Most people call me Brady."

"Sloane Hart. Most people call me Sloane." I turned around and began to walk away.

"See you around, Hart!" he called after me.

~

"Maybe I should text longboard guy and see if they want to come down to post-game," Lauren slurred as we

8

walked into our apartment.

"Why don't we save it? It's only the first night."

"Too late. He replied! He and his roommates are coming down," she interrupted me before I could finish.

"Ooh, I'm manifesting that the other two roommates are just as hot so there's one for each of us!" Jordan laughed.

Lauren pulled out a bottle of tequila, limes and poured each of us a shot. Even though I desperately wanted to go to bed, I knew I couldn't say no.

"Here's to the father, the son, and the tequila chilled. Hope to God this doesn't get us killed. Remember that if he won't, his best friend will. Always remember to take your pill. Now let's go get fucking drilled."

We raised our shot glasses, downed the tequila and quickly followed them up with limes. Seconds later, the front door opened and in walked three tall guys wearing almost identical outfits. I watched as the last of them shut the door behind him. As soon as he turned around, we locked eyes again.

Ethan Brady.

"Guys! This is Graham, Jake and Ethan. They live right above us," Lauren introduced them. Jordan and I awkwardly waved from the kitchen as we grabbed two drinks from the fridge.

Graham looked like he was plucked out of a Billabong campaign. He had shaggy blonde hair, blue eyes and a tan that probably lasted year-round. You could tell he grew up at the beach and had no intention of ever leaving. Jake was the opposite— his dark complexion sported a buzz cut and a little bit of facial hair.

Lauren insisted on making the guys drinks, even

though they came with a full case of Miller Lite. While she did that, Jordan and I got comfortable on the couch and set up a game of Circle of Death.

"Oh, I'm in," Graham joined us.

Everyone made their way to the couch and Jordan reminded us of the rules. Halfway through the first round I excused myself and went to the bathroom. As I walked back down the hall that connected my bedroom to the kitchen, I was stopped by Ethan. His body shifted so that it was blocking me from finding a way out of the hallway and the situation.

"Are you just going to pretend like you don't know me?" he asked.

"I mean, I don't really," I reminded him.

"So that moment back at the bar never happened?"

"If you consider a beer and a two-minute-long conversation a moment, then you probably think this is our first date."

"Good one, but I don't date."

"They never do."

"What's in here?" He brushed past me and let himself into my room.

"My bedroom, obviously." I rolled my eyes.

He looked around the room, picking up picture frames and examining them one by one. I couldn't believe Ethan Brady was in my bedroom. I felt my heart rate increasing by the second and with a newfound drunk confidence, I closed the bedroom door behind me. He looked up and his big brown eyes felt like they could see right through me. Taking the hint, he made his way closer to me and placed one hand on my lower back and the other on my face. Gently, his thumb stroked my cheek, and I could feel the rest of his hand grasp the back of my neck. Goosebumps.

When our lips finally touched, it was like they had met before.

First kisses can be two things: terrible or incredible. My *first* kiss was terrible. I was 15 and it was New Year's Eve. I remember tasting toothpaste on his tongue and thinking he'd brushed his teeth to be courteous. It turns out he was wasted and had been throwing up in the bathroom right before the ball dropped.

Then, there was my first *good* kiss. It was like a scene out of any coming-of-age movie or book made in the past ten years. One Saturday night my senior year of high school, I stayed out past curfew. "Crazy Rap" by Afroman was playing on the Bluetooth speaker while we passed around whiskey and a bottle of Dr. Pepper as a chaser. I knew it was wrong to let Carter drive me home after he drank, but I was 17 and didn't always make the best decisions. He parked his car at the top of my driveway so my parents wouldn't hear the engine, then he kissed me. I can still remember the way my entire body lit up, like I had been going through life on autopilot until that very moment.

That's not what this first kiss with Ethan felt like. Kissing him felt familiar, like our lips were puzzle pieces that fit together just right. He didn't make me nervous in the way Carter used to. He made me feel comfortable. He made me feel at home.

Chapter 2

SLOANE · SEPTEMBER 2016

Lauren started dating Graham Clark three weeks into the semester— which was a lot sooner than I had ever anticipated. Graham and his roommates were all members of the Pi Kappa Alpha fraternity, Pike for short. We'd gone to a few parties over the year, mostly their iconic last day of class (LDOC) parties each semester, but other than that we didn't frequent Pike. With Lauren's new girlfriend title, we started getting invited to everything. I'd be lying if I said I didn't hope to run into Ethan whenever we went to the Pike house. I didn't want to admit to anyone, even myself, that I had feelings for him. I wasn't letting myself fall for anyone during one of the most pivotal years of my life.

Every Wednesday after our morning classes, Lauren, Jordan and I met on the quad and then walked to eat lunch at the food hall. Most seniors didn't eat on campus unless it was a grab-and-go situation, but we started that tradition freshman year so of course we had to see it through. Plus, I'd never turn down Chick-Fil-A.

"What jersey are you guys wearing tonight?" Lauren asked, pulling out a chair from our usual table in the corner.

"Basketball jersey and Converse," Jordan replied.

"Me too," I chimed in.

"Easy enough." Lauren laughed. "I feel like we haven't been to a jersey party in years."

"I think the last one we went to was Pike's. What was that— sophomore year?" Jordan recounted.

"I think you're right, J. Wait, have either of you hooked up with a Pike? If so, do we need to do any damage control before tonight? I just want to be prepared." Lauren was rambling.

We both fell silent for a minute and pulled out our phones to refer to the lists we kept in our notes app.

"Nope," we answered in unison.

"Oh, thank God. I don't want to be the problematic girlfriend." She laughed.

"I wonder if Ethan will be there," I thought out loud.

"Why don't you just text him?" Jordan asked.

"I'm not doing that. I don't want him to think I'm interested or anything."

"Aren't you?" Lauren interjected.

"Well yeah, maybe. It's our senior year though. I don't even know if I'll still be in Wilmington after graduation. Plus, he said it himself— he's not the relationship type. Both of those are pretty good reasons not to get involved with him."

"So what? Sloane, since I met you three years ago the only two guys you've ever talked about have been Carter and Ethan. Don't you want to fall in love? Just have fun! We have an entire year left; so much can happen. I'm gonna ask Graham if Ethan's going tonight." Lauren picked up her phone.

"Wait Laur, don't!" I tried to grab the phone from her.

"Suit yourself," she huffed.

We finished lunch and took the shuttle bus back to Ascent where I worked on a few assignments. After a while, I grabbed my old journal from the drawer in my nightstand, sat on my bed and started flipping through the pages. It was all there— meeting Carter, falling for him and then the inevitable ending. I remember how much the end hurt; at the time I thought I was going to die. Eventually, the pain became so distant that if I hadn't written about it, I would've forgotten it ever happened. Maybe Lauren was right.

I placed the journal back in the drawer and pulled out my new one. It was only a quarter of the way full, and I started it almost two years ago. I tended to write more whenever I experienced extreme emotions— happiness, love, sadness and heartbreak. The journal full of more blank pages than used, told me that maybe I had been extremely empty for the past few years. Maybe it was time to change that.

~

Graham invited us to pregame the jersey party at his apartment, then pledges would sober drive us to the house. I scanned the room for any sign of Ethan when out of the corner of my eye I saw him duck out onto the balcony. I hugged Graham as Jake handed us each a cup of PJ, better known as party juice, which was a concoction of vodka, rum, tequila and a lot of fruit punch.

"You're a Celtics fan?" a voice asked from behind me.

I turned around and was greeted by a very smiley, and

high, Ethan.

"Believe it or not, I found this jersey at Goodwill a few years ago, hours before I came to this very party." I took a sip of PJ.

"Damn, quite a snag. I'm surprised to hear you were at a Pike party though. Maybe we unknowingly met that night," he suggested.

"Yeah, maybe." I shrugged in agreement even though I know we didn't meet that night. I would've never forgotten him.

"Yo, Brady," Graham interrupted us. "Pledges are pulling up, you're in our car." We followed him to the parking lot where a line of cars was waiting.

"Lap up!" Jake instructed Ethan, Graham, Lauren, Jordan and I as he took the front seat. Jordan sandwiched herself in the middle as Lauren took her place on Graham's lap, which was when I realized I'd have to do the same.

"Watch your head," Ethan said as I crouched down and swung my legs over his. He closed the door and rested one hand on my thigh and the other on my lower back.

When we walked into the party together, it felt like we were *together*. The house was just like you'd expect any place occupied by a few 20-something-year-old guys would look. Beer cans and empty liquor bottles were scattered on the floor that was already coated in a layer of stickiness from the last party. Ethan led me to a keg on the back porch and introduced me to every person we passed. I felt important and I never wanted the night to end.

"Thanks for the drink." I smiled. "I need to go find the girls."

"I'll come. I'm gonna see if Graham wants to run the

pong table with me."

We made our way back through the party and into the kitchen where we found Lauren and Graham playing beer pong. Moments later I saw Jordan sitting on the counter in the kitchen talking to a guy I didn't recognize. So much for finding the girls. Instead of interrupting either of them, I stayed by Ethan's side.

"We've got next game," he bent down and whispered in my ear.

"I feel like I should warn you that I kind of suck. Flip cup is more my thing."

"Well then I want you on my team for that too."

"Let's gooooo!" Graham held up his cup and chugged it to let everyone in the room know that he won— again. "Brady, you up next?"

Ethan guided me to the other side of the table by taking my hand. We rearranged the cups while I filled them with my keg beer.

"Be right back," he mouthed. Shortly, he returned with two fresh drinks. "Alright let's do this."

To no one's surprise, we lost. I weaved in and out of the crowd until I got to the living room to see if Jordan had relocated. After a few minutes and no luck finding her, I checked my phone to see that she told the group chat she was leaving. I called an Uber and headed onto the front porch when Ethan stopped me in the foyer.

"Leaving already?" he asked.

"Yeah, thinking about it. Jordan left and I really don't want to spend the night hovering around the pong table by myself," I explained.

"Why don't we go back to my place? I have some weed and I bet there's leftover PJ. Then you won't have to pay for a ride."

"Are you sure? You don't have to leave with me."

"I know I don't have to. I want to." He grabbed my hand and led me outside.

~

When we got back to Ascent, we were greeted by a shit show of an apartment.

"This is disgusting." I scrunched my nose.

"It's alright, we can leave it. Graham, Jake and I will worry about it in the morning."

"How can you sleep knowing this mess is outside of your door? We just need a trash bag and some paper towels; it'll take us ten minutes tops."

"If you insist, Hart."

Ethan blasted a 2000's rap playlist on the speaker and handed me a trash bag. I started collecting any empty cup or beer can that resided on the counter, while he followed wiping down every surface. Once we finished cleaning, he poured us each a cup of PJ and led me out to the balcony where we sat in two folding chairs overlooking the pool.

"Want a hit?" he asked, picking up a bong off the ground.

"No thanks, I don't smoke," I replied.

"Never?" He seemed surprised.

"Never," I assured him.

"So, then what do you do to relax?"

"Umm," I thought for a minute. "Binge Netflix or write."

"What do you write about?"

"A lot of things. I freelance for a few publications to make some extra money, so those pieces are usually more news and culture based. But when I write for fun it's more like journaling— putting my feelings on paper. What about you? What do you do for fun?"

"Sports," he said almost instantly. "I played football my entire life and got a full ride to go to college for it, but it just didn't work out. Now I just watch a lot of sports and coach kids part-time at the YMCA."

"Do you coach football?"

"In the fall, yeah, but in the spring, I also do soccer and baseball. It's easy since they're all under 12 years old."

"Do you have younger siblings?"

"I'm an only child." He took another hit from the bong.

"Me too. I wish I had siblings though, like a big family. Have you ever watched *Shameless*? They're the least functional TV family, but there's never a dull moment. I feel like that'd be more fun than the loneliness I felt growing up." I knew I was drunk by the way I started rambling.

"I get that. I've known Graham since first grade, we got close so him and his brother became like family to me." He fell silent for a second. "So *Shameless*, should we watch?"

My heart was pounding in my chest as Ethan led me through the apartment and into his room. I chugged the rest of my drink and placed it on his dresser. I was in Ethan Brady's bedroom. The room he slept in. The room that knew all of his deepest darkest secrets. I was standing in the middle of it. His bed was placed in the same spot as mine, in the corner against the wall. He had a navy blue comforter with matching striped sheets and a Patriots poster hung above the headboard.

I took a seat on the edge of his bed and unlaced my

high-top sneakers as he flicked through Netflix to find the show. He sat upright so that his back was flush with the headboard and patted the mattress as if he wanted me to sit next to him.

"You like this show?" he asked a few minutes into the first episode when someone's bare butt came across the screen.

"We can shut it off," I laughed awkwardly. "I forgot there was some nudity."

"Nudity. So formal."

The show continued to play while he turned to face me. I did the same. We stared at each other as I took in every detail of him. His long eyelashes, the freckles on his nose, the way he licked his lips when he was nervous. Then, he leaned in to kiss me. Our mouths became one again and I felt more at home than I'd ever been. My tongue followed his motions as his hand made its way to my back and up my shirt. We didn't go any further and even though every ounce of me wanted to. I liked that we were taking it slow.

~

I woke up fully clothed on top of Ethan's comforter. His arm was draped over my stomach and the sound of light snoring filled the room. I quietly wiggled my way out from under him and grabbed my shoes before sneaking out of his apartment. I couldn't risk getting caught by either of our roommates.

The alarm clock on my nightstand read 7:45 a.m. so I changed into pajamas and climbed back into my bed to make up for the hours of sleep I lost the night before. As I drifted off, I replayed everything over again in my head. I was falling for Ethan Brady, and I couldn't stop myself. I didn't want to.

Chapter 3

ETHAN · SEPTEMBER 2016

I opened my eyes to an empty bed, expecting to find Sloane next to me. Hoping to wake up to her freckled nose and hazel eyes, I was disappointed to realize she snuck out on me. After a few groggy minutes, I picked up my phone to check the time. It was barely 9 a.m. which meant I had at least another two hours before the guys would drag my ass to the gym. I ripped off my shirt, threw it on the ground and got under the sheets. I hated sleeping with clothes on.

"Dude, get up." Graham burst through the door.

"Knock much?" I groan.

"We have to be at the house for philanthropy shit, remember?" He was gone before I could even argue. Reluctantly, I got out of bed and made my way into the shower.

We pulled up to the fraternity house and the parking lot was packed. It was Pike's annual volleyball tournament. All the sororities always came to cheer us on and pledge money to their favorite teams. Usually, I looked forward to this day every year but considering I got about five hours of sleep last night, I knew I was gonna embarrass myself out there.

"Brady, let's go!" Jake waved from the court.

Shit, we were first up?

Sports had been a part of my life for as long as I could remember. When my dad wasn't at work, he would toss a football with me in the front yard until the sun went down. Graham and I played on the same recreational soccer team until middle school, when I signed up for football. I could've gone to college to play, I almost did. I got a few offers from out-of-state schools, but the tuition was insane, and they weren't full rides. Instead, I chose to end my football career, stay close to home and attend Wilmington College alongside Graham.

I tossed my sneakers to the side of the court and took my spot in the sand. We won the first game and when we had a ten-minute break to grab water, I noticed Sloane and Lauren sitting in the grass behind another group of girls.

"Looks like we have at least two fans, fellas." Jake must've caught me staring because he waved to them.

"Hey babe!" Lauren called out to Graham.

I smiled at Sloane and when she returned the favor something in me felt... different? I tried to shake it off as I got my head back into the game, but I felt myself glancing in her direction whenever I could. We lost the next game, probably due to my newfound distraction.

After the game, I made my rounds, grabbed a mimosa and took a seat on the beach towel next to Sloane, Graham and Lauren.

"You guys did great! Well, for the first game at least." Lauren laughed.

"Like you could've played better," Graham countered. "You peaced out early last night, Brady. Where'd you go? You missed us running the pong table."

"Oh, believe me, I caught plenty of that. I went back to Ascent and just smoked a little," I replied, avoiding eye contact with Sloane.

"You're both so lame. Sloane went home early too," Lauren interjected. "You should've shared a ride; I hate when she Ubers alone."

Out of the corner of my eye, I saw a smirk appear on Sloane's face. God, she's even cuter when she's uncomfortable. Her cheeks turn a shade of pink I've never seen before and she can't stop the corners of her mouth from turning upward, unveiling a big toothy grin. Fuck. Was I staring at her? I turned my attention back to the game for the next half hour and made sure not to look in Sloane's direction again. Instead, I got in my own head.

What was last night? It wasn't a one-night stand, I mean we didn't even hook up. I wanted to, though. I wanted to more than I thought I did. Something about her tells me that she didn't do casual hookups though and I knew I couldn't handle more than that right now, or probably ever.

"You guys wanna grab lunch at Jerry's?" Graham interrupted my train of thought.

"Let's make moves, I'm starving," I replied.

"You heard the guy. Jerry's it is." Graham stood up and reached out for Lauren's hand to help her up. It took everything in me not to do the same for Sloane.

I followed the three of them to the gate that led to the parking lot and dapped up a few brothers on our way out. Lauren took the passenger seat, so Sloane and I sat in the back of Graham's Jeep.

"Should we have asked Jake to come?" Sloane looked at me. "I'm assuming he rode here with you guys?"

"He's probably gonna sub in; somehow he's been on the winning team every year." I shrugged.

"Fucking Jake, who would've thought," Graham laughed. "The dude plays video games all day long, you'd never know he had an athletic bone in his body."

We got to Jerry's just as the 4 p.m. football games were starting so it was packed. Somehow, we still managed to grab four seats next to each other at the bar. Graham and I sat on either side of Lauren and Sloane so they could talk to each other, forcing me to either start a conversation with Sloane or watch the games.

"Why'd you run off this morning?" I lowered my voice.

"I, um, just thought it would be less awkward that way," she explained nervously. "Plus, sleeping on top of your comforter in my clothes from last night wasn't exactly very comfortable."

"You could've gotten under them." I placed my hand on her leg. She shot me a look that said *what the fuck are you doing* and then removed my hand. I could tell she liked it though.

Since the day that I met her, I'd thought about kissing Sloane every time that I saw her. That moment was no different. I stared at her mouth and swallowed heavy. My eyes shifted from her mouth to her eyes. I knew that she knew what I wanted. I also knew she wanted it too.

"What're you both ordering?" Lauren curiously leaned over the bar.

"Buffalo chicken wrap," Sloane and I said in unison.

She whipped her head around so fast that her long red hair brushed my bicep. I winked and then she turned her attention back to Lauren as I ordered the four of us a bucket of beers.

~

By 8 p.m. I was down on my bets and behind on my assignments. When we got back to Ascent, we said bye to Sloane and Lauren, then Graham and I walked up the extra flight of stairs to our place.

"Cowboys game?" he asked.

"Can't. I have a few assignments due at midnight."

"So, what's going on with Sloane?"

The question caught me off-guard.

"What do you mean?"

"Dude, don't act like I haven't known you for over a decade. I can tell you're into her. Have the two of you hooked up? I won't tell Lauren."

"Fuck off. But to answer your question— no, we haven't hooked up." I slammed my bedroom door in his face and flopped onto my bed.

Maybe I was fucked. Was it really that obvious that I was attracted to her? That would make for an extremely tough year. I lifted myself up off the bed and sat down at my desk. I couldn't fall behind less than a month into the semester or I'd get kicked out of the business program.

It was almost midnight by the time I finished everything. I showered, got into bed and was about to turn on my alarm for my 8 a.m. class when Sloane's name appeared in my notifications. I felt a smile form on my face.

Yep, I was fucked.

Chapter 4

SLOANE · OCTOBER 2016

I anxiously sat in class waiting for the professor to pass out our creative writing midterm. On the last two assignments, I scored lower than I would've liked to, which made me realize that I was struggling creatively. If I couldn't write a simple assignment for a writing class, how was I supposed to land a job at major media publication one day? That's what every day working there would be like— ideating, writing and publishing. I stared at the clock above the door and watched as he made his way around the room, handing us each a different prompt. I could feel my throat tighten.

After the exam, it felt like a weight was lifted off my shoulders, at least until I received the grade back. I placed the blue book on the front table and left class. I plugged my earbuds into my phone and shuffled Spotify's Top Hits playlist. "Closer" by The Chainsmokers played as I made my way across campus to the parking lot where the shuttle bus took us back to Ascent. I felt my phone vibrate in my pocket and was surprised to see Ethan's name on the screen. I hadn't heard from him in a few weeks. I was sure that flame had burnt out.

Ethan Brady: Turn around.

There he was. I stopped and waited for him to reach where I was standing in the quad—even the way he walked was arrogant. Why did I kind of like it though?

"Hey Hart," he greeted me with that stupid grin of his.

"You mean Sloane," I replied. "Are you on your way to a midterm?"

"Nope, just finished my last one so I'm heading back to the apartment. What about you?" he asked.

"Me too." I sighed.

"Don't sound so depressed now." He nudged me.

"It's not that I'm not excited for midterms to be over. I'm just not doing as well as I'd like in my creative writing class, which sucks because it's the one class that's most like the field I want to go into. How am I going to get hired if I can't even write something decent?"

"It sounds like you're being hard on yourself. I'm sure they're great. You know what they say— you're always your harshest critic."

I didn't expect Ethan Brady to be good at giving advice, but then again, he'd exceeded all expectations I had for him.

"Thanks, I needed that."

"What're you doing for fall break?"

"Staying here; lame, I know," I answered. "I just don't see the point of going home while my mom works the entire weekend and I watch Netflix alone in her living room. I can do that here. What about you?"

"Me too." Ethan shrugged.

We waited for the shuttle to pull up and without question sat next to each other. Even if it were in silence, it was a comfortable silence.

~

"Sloane?" Lauren called out from her room.

"Yeah?" I replied.

"Can you come here?" She sounded concerned.

I made my way through the kitchen and down the front hall where her bedroom was. A suitcase was on her floor, and it seemed as though her entire wardrobe was in a pile on her bed.

"What is going on here?" I laughed.

"Don't laugh, it's bad, I know." She put her head in her hands. "Graham wants me to meet his parents this weekend and I don't know what to pack. He said they're chill but they're literally millionaires. Can you help?"

"Just be yourself!" I sat crisscross next to the suitcase and examined what she had packed.

After an hour, we had seven outfits picked for a four-day trip— just in case. I was excited for Lauren. I'd never seen her that happy because of a guy and I knew Graham was a good one.

"When do you leave?" I asked. "And where's Jordan?"

"She left while you were at class, something about picking up an extra shift tonight. I'm supposed to be at his apartment... Shit, five minutes ago."

"Go, go, go." I stood up.

"You're sure you'll be okay by yourself all weekend? I feel bad leaving you." Lauren pouted.

"Yes, I'll be fine! I'm going to write. I desperately need some creative inspiration." I followed her out of the room and waved her off.

"Goodbye my little writer. Love ya!"

The door shut behind her and the silence in the apartment was deafening. What *was* I going to do for the next four days? Surely, I couldn't write that much. I sat on the couch and put an old episode of *Keeping Up with the Kardashians* on the TV. For dinner, I cooked a box of Kraft macaroni and cheese and poured myself a glass of Moscato. Is this what living alone post-grad would be like? I kind of liked it. I scrolled through Instagram and then Snapchat before checking my texts, where I was surprised to see I had missed a message from Ethan.

Ethan Brady: Wanna watch that nudist show?

He wanted to hang out with me? He wanted to hang out with me! I replied right away since it had already been an hour and darted to my bathroom to freshen up. Fifteen minutes later, he was in my living room.

"You brought vodka? Are you trying to get me wasted tonight?" I asked.

"I didn't want to come empty handed, and this is all we had." He held up the bottle of American Vodka.

"Do you like wine? I mean, that is if you consider Moscato wine."

"Sure, I'll try it."

"We don't have to watch *Shameless*, you know," I said from the kitchen. "You can pick something else out."

I sat so close to him on the couch that our legs were almost touching. We decided on a new movie that had just released starring Zac Efron, and he got up to shut off the lights.

"It's the only way I can watch movies," he explained, even though I didn't argue.

Halfway through the movie, the wine made me feel a little fuzzy and with that same tipsy confidence as last time, I rested my hand on his thigh. In response, he put his arm around me and pulled me in closer. The next thing I knew, Ethan's mouth crashed over mine.

That kiss was different than the ones that came before. That kiss was pure hunger. His hand caressed my hip and eventually the other hand found its way under my shirt. My heart was pounding, and I knew he could feel it. I brought my mouth to his neck and then his ear.

"Should we go to my room?"

Within seconds he was standing, and as soon as I followed suit, he picked me up. I wrapped my legs around his waist, and we kissed the entire way to my bedroom. When we got inside, I expected him to put me on the bed but instead, he pressed me up against the wall and kissed me even harder. I could feel how turned on he was as he pressed himself into me. After a few minutes, he laid me down and tried to get on top of me.

"My turn," I said, and he didn't argue.

I wrapped my arms around the back of his neck and kissed him gently at first. As our motions became heavier, some of our clothes came off. I stopped him when his hand got to the waistband of my leggings.

"I don't think I want to, you know, yet."

"Oh yeah, of course."

As much as I really wanted to have all of him in that moment, I didn't. I already knew I was in too deep and if we went any further, I thought I just might drown.

~

Lauren and Jordan got home early on Sunday, and we were all eager to catch up. As we settled into a table at Dockside, the smell of saltwater wafted through the air, and I breathed a sigh of relief. I was so glad to have them home. Dockside had become our go-to spot for weekend debriefs and it was one of my favorite traditions that we had.

"Alright Laur, out with it. How'd the weekend with the fam go?" Jordan asked.

"Yeah, you didn't even text the group chat with updates!" I added.

"Don't freak out, but I think I'm in love." Lauren's face turned bright red, and I knew she wasn't kidding, even though she used a playful tone.

"Spill."

"I love his parents, especially his mom. I mean she is just so cool. I sat by the pool with her while the boys fished, and we drank expensive wine while she told me story after story. How she met Graham's dad, wild college parties, what she did post-grad, all of it. I literally aspire to be her. Enough about me though; how was everyone else's weekend?"

"Yeah, what'd you get into J?" I asked.

"I landed a serving gig on a yacht down in Charleston. We made so much in tips, it was insane. Plus, they let us drink whatever we wanted the entire time and I was with some of my high school friends, so it didn't really feel like work."

"Both sound like such glamorous weekends, I'm jealous. Ascent wasn't the same without you guys," I replied.

"Did you get a lot of writing done?" Lauren asked as

the server set down our drinks.

"Actually, I didn't write at all."

"What'd you do then?"

"Hung out with Ethan. Pretty much every night."

"You banged Ethan?!" Lauren shouted.

"Shut up, no! We watched movies, drank wine and had a few sleepovers."

"Okay but, like, what did the sleepovers entail?"

"I'm not saying it out loud!"

"Prude." Lauren laughed. "So, no sex? Why not? We all know you're into each other, it's written all over both of your faces anytime you're in the same room."

"Laur, I've told you like a hundred times. I don't want a boyfriend. We graduate in like…" I paused and counted from October to May on my fingers. "Seven months. Of course, I like him but I'm afraid if I sleep with him, I'll just end up getting more hurt in the end. I really don't want to go through the Carter thing all over again."

"Oh, boohoo, Sloane. So, you slept with a guy, and it didn't work out. It wasn't the end of the world, was it? It's not like you haven't hooked up with anyone since Carter; why can't you treat this like one of those times?"

"Because it's not like one of those times. Honestly, it's not even like Carter. I've never felt this way about anyone before and it scares me. Plus, we all know I can't separate feelings from sex."

"But you can fool around? I'm not following."

"She's right, Sloane," Jordan jumped in. "You're hurting yourself either way. Not having sex with him won't fix anything at this point. It's kind of like an all-or-nothing situation."

I hated that they were right.

31

Chapter 5

SLOANE · DECEMBER 2016

The last day of fall semester fell on a Wednesday. It was one of those December nights that felt cold enough to snow, even though it never would. Classes were finally over, which meant there was only one semester of senior year left. There were only 15 short weeks until I would be catapulted into adulthood. Lauren was still spending almost every waking moment with Graham but unfortunately for me I hadn't seen much of Ethan since fall break.

Some could say that was a good thing, considering I didn't want to get attached, but the way I felt about Ethan made me question everything. Not hearing from him for months after we spent an entire weekend together was definitely a little gut-wrenching. I tried to my hardest to hide my hurt and continue as if fall break had never happened. Just like he seemed to be doing.

In true Thursday fashion, we kicked off the night at a Pike pregame before we made our way to Jerry's. I felt a rush to my head as I slid off the barstool and found my way to the bathroom. After I made a few new friends in line, I weaved in and out of the crowded bar until I felt a hand on my shoulder. Expecting it to be Lauren, I was surprised when my gaze met Ethan's.

"Let's go." He motioned toward a back door, and I don't know why but I followed him.

"Where are we going?" I asked.

"Home."

We started walking toward the bridge and even though I was hoping he'd called an Uber since it was below freezing out, the thought of having more time with him cancelled out the numbness in my toes.

"So, how'd the rest of your semester go? Are you ready to graduate?"

"Don't remind me." I rolled my eyes. "It's been okay, I got my grade up in creative writing. How about you? I haven't seen you around much."

"Yeah, I've been dealing with some stuff, so I haven't had as much time to go out as I'd like."

"What kind of stuff?" I caught myself before he could reply. "Sorry, you don't need to tell me. Forget I asked."

He paused for a moment as if he were contemplating whether-or-not he trusted me. "My scholarship fell through. I was able to get a grant and financial aid for most of it, but I had to cover the rest."

"Gosh that must've been tough. Where do you work?"

"I bartend at a golf course. I love it, honestly."

We walked quietly, hand in hand, until we made it over the bridge. Ethan pulled out his phone and I hope that he was getting us a ride.

"Uber's here. He's that black Ford."

"Oh, thank god, I thought I was going to freeze to

death!"

"Maybe you should've worn pants." He tugged at the oversized sweater that I'd worn as a dress.

Pike's first semester LDOC party was always holiday themed, so it was a tradition to wear an ugly Christmas sweater. I borrowed one of Lauren's and paired it with some over-the-knee boots and a choker necklace. For someone who didn't have anything to wear twenty minutes before the pregame, I was impressed with the outcome.

The driver pulled up to the front gate and let us out. We were greeted by two security officers who buzzed us through, and we walked through the parking lot toward our building.

"So, Hart, mine or yours?"

My entire life I'd only ever been called Sloane and that was the third time since we met that he'd called me Hart. When he used the nickname, I felt like the most important person in the room— or in this case, parking lot.

"Yours." That's when he kissed me.

After a few minutes, he pulled away and led me up all three flights of stairs, stopping at his front door to kiss me again. We walked through a dark, empty apartment and went straight to his bedroom. Taking a seat on the edge of his bed, I untied my boots and wiggled them off. I watched as he placed his wallet and watch on the nightstand. He was so particular about everything he did. Even the simplest movements taught me so much about him. We made our way under the covers, like they were our new favorite place. I nestled my body, still in the ugly Christmas sweater, into his.

Ethan smelled like Old Spice. His hands grazed my

lower back as mine were intertwined in his hair. I nuzzled my face into his shoulder as he kissed my neck and then found his way back to my mouth. I was taking in every second of this moment. It was one I never wanted to forget.

"I'm ready," I whispered.

~

Light just barely seeped through his broken blinds, which meant wasn't even 7:30 a.m. yet. I rolled over to face Ethan as he wrapped his arms around me and pulled my body as close to his as it could get. I laid my head on his bare chest and admired the freckles that covered his upper body. We started kissing easily, like waking up together was something we'd done hundreds of times before.

"I'm glad you're here."

I relished the words. They were all I had wanted to hear for months. They let me know that maybe I wasn't making a mistake by taking a chance on him.

"Me too." I smiled.

That moment was my undoing. Ethan Brady had me. As much as I didn't want to admit it, he was holding my bare heart in his hands. I was so afraid of what he might do to it, but I also couldn't wait to find out.

"Where'd you disappear to last night?" Lauren asked as I walked through the door.

"Caught you red handed!" Jordan chimed in. "Kidding, but really tell us everything."

Before I could even have a conversation, I knew I needed to eat. I took a seat at the kitchen counter and dug my hand into the bag of bagels that sat in front of me.

"We slept together," I admitted.

"You say it like it's a bad thing." Lauren seemed confused. "Was it bad?"

"No," I started. "It was good, like too good."

"See, this is good!" Lauren took my bagel and put it in the toaster oven with hers. "This is what we'd call making progress. Right, J?"

"No tea, no shade, just facts," Jordan replied.

Lauren and I both looked at her like she had five heads.

"Did you hear that from one of your reality shows?"

"Never say that again."

We all laughed and ate breakfast together before we had to lock ourselves in our rooms to study for finals. My phone vibrated on the counter as I washed the last of our dishes.

"Is it Ethan?" Jordan asked, trying to peek at the screen.

"Jordan!" I quickly picked up my phone.

From the way a smile formed on my face, they both knew it was him. I took my phone, went to my room and opened my journal for the first time in months. I was excited about someone again. I forgot how good this felt. Even though I had no business getting into a relationship with one semester of school left, Ethan felt worth the risk. Something about him made me picture a future.

I replied to his text and to my surprise we kept the conversation going for days. After finals were over, we spent the night together again, and again, and again until we were together pretty much every single night.

~

Everyone went home for the entire three-week-long winter break except for Ethan and me. We stayed in Wilmington for most of it, only going back for Christmas

Eve and Day. We hadn't talked much about what we were or if we were dating, but to me it felt like it. We were just as much of a couple as Graham and Lauren, minus the label.

"Hibachi or pizza tonight?" I asked.

The wine cork made a popping sound as I poured us each a glass of Pinot Noir. Over the past few weeks, Ethan and I were training our palates to like wine because I refused to turn 22 and only drink Moscato.

"What's supposed to pair better with red?" He paused his video game and joined me in the kitchen.

"Uh, I think steak? But that's a little out of our budget."

"Hibachi it is." He came up from behind me, placed his hands on my waist and mouth on my neck.

"Taste this one." I spun around. "Tell me what you think."

"This might be my new favorite. I just hate the way red wine stains my lips."

"I like it." I reached up and rubbed my thumb over his bottom lip.

He brushed a piece of hair out of my face and then kissed me. I liked the way the wine tasted on his tongue better than in my glass. We ordered dinner, finished the bottle of Pinot and a movie before calling it a night.

"How bad is it if I don't go upstairs to brush my teeth?" he asked.

"I have an unopened toothbrush you can use."

"The old toothbrush trick, huh?"

"Oh, shut up." I shoved the packaging into his chest.

I ran mine under the stream of cold water and spread some toothpaste on it before I handed him the tube. We brushed in silence, staring at one another in the mirror and eventually erupted into a fit of laughter. Ethan pulled his phone from the waistband of his gym shorts and started taking a video of us. That's when I knew he was just as invested in this as I was.

When we got into bed, our bodies found their way to their usual positions— Ethan laid on his back, while I was curled up into him with my head on his chest.

"The past few weeks have felt like we've lived together, kind of." I pointed out.

"Have they?" He chuckled.

"I just meant that we've spent a lot of time together lately. I've never spent this many days consecutively with someone and not hate them."

"Yeah, I guess you're right. Me too."

"When was your last relationship?" The words spewed out of me before I could stop them.

"Uh," he thought for a moment. "I dated a girl briefly in high school, if you count that. It was for like three months or something."

I didn't say anything.

"What about you? When was yours?"

"Never," I replied as it if it were instinctual. "It was hard to make friends, let alone get a boyfriend when I moved around so much. Then my parents split, I moved into college and, well, I think I've kind of been afraid."

"I get that."

Neither one of us spoke for the next few minutes. I thought there was a chance he might be asleep when I said, "I've never felt this way about anyone."

"Me either," he replied.

He wrapped me in his arms, and it felt like I was home.

Then he kissed me like he wanted me to remember that kiss, like he never wanted me to forget him. As if he were easily forgettable. I imagine that I'll never be able to forget him.

~

New Year's Eve would be the first time we stepped out together as more than just neighbors. With all our friends back in town, I was thrilled for the night ahead.

Standing in front of my bathroom mirror, wearing a robe and a towel on my head, I couldn't help but notice how much more confident I was. My smile was brighter, my skin was clearer, and my heart was happier. I pulled a drug store liquid eyeliner out of my makeup bag and applied a heavy layer to my eyelids, followed by two coats of mascara.

"Are you almost ready?" Lauren peered through the doorway. "You look hot! Do you think Ethan's going to ask you to be his girlfriend tonight? You've always said you wanted a New Year's Eve proposal."

"Have I ever told you how annoying you are?" I joked. "But no, we haven't talked about it yet."

"What *have* you talked about?" Does he like you? Are you just hooking up? Don't you want to know? It's basically eating me alive over here. I can't imagine being you."

"Of course, I want to know. I know he likes me. He's told me that. We haven't talked about much else, but it's more than just sex. I can feel it. You know?" I turned to look at Lauren, whose facial expression told me that she didn't agree with anything I just said.

"I don't know, Sloane. Graham told me that the entire time he's known Ethan, which has been like over ten years or something, he's never dated anyone. I just don't want you to get hurt."

"So, I can't be the first?"

"You know I didn't mean it like that," she replied. "I'm sorry I said anything. Let's just have a good night.

"We will. Things are good with Ethan and I right now; I don't see a reason to change them."

"If you're happy, I'm happy."

Part of me agreed with the words that were coming out of my mouth but another part of me knew they weren't necessarily true.

"Let's go ladies, Ubers are here!" Graham yelled from the living room.

We joined the guys for one last shot before we started getting charged by the driver. Ethan handed me a shot glass and we clinked ours together in honor of the new year. I had a feeling it was going to be a good one.

"You're in my Uber, Hart."

I followed Ethan into an SUV and sat on his lap so we could fit everyone in two cars. It reminded me of one of the first nights we spent together. I'd give almost anything to go back to that night and tell them what we knew now, so we could have even more time together.

When we got to the party, Ethan and I were glued at the hip. We mingled with our roommates and some of his brothers and their girlfriends, but we mostly kept to ourselves until Graham called us into the dining room for a game of flip cup.

"You two have to split up," he said. "We need one more on each team."

"Oh, you're on. Didn't you say you were great at this game?" Ethan winked at me.

"Great might've been an exaggeration." I laughed.

"Match up!"

An hour later, it was 11:58 p.m. and everyone was gathering in the living room to watch the ball drop. I was nestled under Ethan's arm, exactly where I wanted to end that year and start the next.

"Three, two, one... Happy New Year!" everyone shouted in sync.

Ethan grabbed me with a little bit of force and placed his mouth on mine. He kissed me harder than he ever had before. Everyone around us cheered and hugged, but we couldn't pull away from each other.

"Happy New Year."

We were good and we didn't need a title to tell us that. I took what I could get with Ethan because even though it had only been a few weeks, I couldn't imagine life without him. I hoped that I would never have to.

Chapter 6

SLOANE · JANUARY 2017

Just like that, it was our final semester of college. Four years had come and gone in the blink of an eye. It felt like just yesterday when my parents, who weren't on speaking terms at the time, dropped me off at Moore Hall and I cried while eating microwaveable popcorn for dinner. I wasn't much for regrets, but I wished that I could rewind time. I wasn't ready to leave Wilmington, or Ethan. The only thing I could do was make the most of the time I had left.

Thanks to Martin Luther King Jr. we had a long weekend and Graham invited us to spend it at his family's cabin in Asheville. It was like our own little mountain weekend. The drive there was long and terrifying. I closed my eyes the entire way up the Blue Ridge Parkway, not only because I thought Jake might run us off the road, but I was also terrified of heights. When we finally pulled into the driveway, I opened my eyes and was blown away by the sight in front of me.

When Graham said his parents owned a cabin in the

mountains, I was expecting just that— a cabin. The house was perched on a slope, surrounded by a lot of trees. The house was three stories tall with a warm wooden exterior and large windows, which I'm sure offered gorgeous views.

"Wow," I said to Ethan as he grabbed my bag from the trunk.

"Nice, right?"

Nice was an understatement. The house looked like it was taken straight out of a magazine. We entered on the bottom floor, which seemed to be a recreational area. It was an open, yet inviting space with a bar, pool table and living room that featured a large stone fireplace, sectional couch and TV that I knew the guys would watch the playoffs on.

"You guys made it!" Lauren ran down the stairs to hug us.

"I was almost positive we were going to die on the drive up here." I laughed. "I kept my eyes closed for the last thirty minutes."

"Oh, I did the same. Let's put your bags down and make some drinks!" Jordan and I followed her up to the main living area while the guys finished unpacking the car.

I took in every detail as we made our way through the house. The ceilings were stained wood with low-bearing beams and the walls were off-white. Sliding glass doors and windows covered the back wall and you could see mountain tops for miles. All I could think about was what it would be like to be that successful one day. My parents never struggled, but we were never well-off enough for a second home or international vacations.

43

"Should we make some bloodies?" Lauren asked, waving around a bottle of Grey Goose.

"You know I love a good bloody!" Jordan was practically drooling.

"I have a love-hate relationship with them. I love the first few sips and then hate the rest," I replied.

We made a pitcher anyway and sat at the island that was at least ten feet long, while we went over the agenda for the weekend.

"Okay, so we'll spend today at the house. We're having groceries delivered, we can drink, play games and go in the hot tub. Tomorrow we're skiing, Sunday is football and then Monday we'll be on our way home!" Lauren recited from a note in her phone.

~

By the end of the night, the six of us found our way into the hot tub each with a glass of whiskey— which was very uncommon for me.

"Should we play never have I ever?" Lauren asked.

"Sloane's favorite game!" Jordan laughed. The boys rolled their eyes, and then willingly held up ten fingers.

"Never have I ever smoked weed," I started off the game and everyone put down a finger.

"Come on, that's always your go-to!" Lauren argued.

"Well, it works, doesn't it?"

"Maybe we should change that. Jake, get the bong," Graham ordered.

"I'm good," I declined. Jake passed it around anyway and everyone else took a hit.

"Never have I ever been a high school athlete." Lauren knew that would get all the guys and Jordan. Somehow, I almost always ended up winning this game. Did that make me boring?

It was Graham's turn. "Never have I ever cheated on someone."

Jake and Ethan both put down a finger. I could feel my stomach get uneasy as a pit started to form in my throat. I needed to remove myself from the situation, stat.

"I'm going to the bathroom." I quickly grabbed a towel and made my way inside.

After I finally located a bathroom, I locked the door and leaned over the sink until I felt tears rolling down my face. Why was I so upset? It wasn't like he cheated on me, I mean he couldn't cheat on me since we weren't dating, it was just something that happened in his past. It made me feel like I didn't know him, though.

"Sloane?" Ethan knocked. "Open up."

"I just need a second." I sniffled.

To conceal the fact that I was crying, I flushed the toilet before letting him in. When I turned the doorknob, I avoided looking at him until he took hold of my chin and directed my gaze towards him.

"I'm sorry." His thumb brushed my cheek, wiping away a tear. "I didn't realize you'd get so upset. It was the girl I told you about from high school. I was barely 16, you can imagine how young and stupid I was back then."

"I might have overreacted a little, I'm just scared. This whole thing between us scares me, and I really don't want to get hurt."

"I wouldn't hurt you, Sloane." He pulled my body into his and rested his chin on my head. "I'm scared too."

I looked up at Ethan and saw sincerity and regret written all over his face. I knew he was telling the truth. We walked back outside to join the group, hand in hand.

I still felt scared, but I had no reason not to trust him. So, I had to try. One by one, everyone started to trickle out of the hot tub and to their rooms. Ethan and I were the last two standing.

"Carry me upstairs?" I asked.

"Get on, Hart." He secured the towel around his waist and bent down so I could jump on his back. Nervously, I grabbed his shoulders, and he hoisted me up. When we finally reached the third floor, Ethan kicked the door shut and dropped me backwards onto the bed.

"You're beautiful. You know that right?" He stared at me.

In just my bathing suit and a towel, I felt somewhat exposed. My face went flush as he opened the towel and continued to devour me with his eyes. Ethan made his way on top of me and started to kiss every inch of my body. Usually that made me feel uncomfortable, but this time I let him. He brought out a confidence in me that I'd never felt with anyone else.

"Maybe take these off though." He tugged at my earrings and laughed a little.

"What do you have against jewelry?" I asked while I obeyed his request.

"I just think you look better without it."

I placed my earrings on the nightstand, made my way under the covers as Ethan followed. Our bodies found their way to each other like they did most nights.

"I want you," he whispered.

Little did he know, he already had all of me.

~

In the middle of the night, I rolled over to readjust my sleeping position and realized that Ethan wasn't next to me. I reached for my phone to check the time and see if he'd texted to tell me where he was going. No new notifications except for a comment from a classmate on my discussion board post. I got out of bed and grabbed a t-shirt and sweatpants out of my duffle bag before heading downstairs to find him.

After a few minutes of scoping out the main level, I noticed one of the back sliding doors was ajar. I found him sitting in a rocking chair, staring at the electric fire he must've started.

"Hey," I said sitting down in the chair next to him. "Are you okay?"

Ethan was silent for a minute.

"I just needed some space."

"From me?"

"No, from this house, that bedroom. It's hard being back here sometimes."

"Why?"

"It just brings up a lot of memories that I've tried to forget and don't want to re-live. I spent so much of my childhood here— Thanksgiving, Christmas, New Year's Eve— I think that's why I hate most holidays," he confessed. "The Clarks are great people, but it was hard to be surrounded by this perfect family that wasn't mine. It was just a constant reminder that I'd never have that."

"I'm sorry," I tried to offer support instead of asking more questions.

"Don't be sorry, it's not your fault." He reached across the chair and placed his hand on mine. "Go back to bed, I'll be up in a little."

Reluctantly, I listened. When I got back to our room and was nestled under the covers, I wondered what really happened to him when he was younger. How bad could it have been? Clearly bad enough to scare him out of falling in love. Even though my parents were divorced, I still believed that love existed. It's never perfect, never secure and sometimes never forever. But it's something that I believe everyone should experience at least once in their life.

Chapter 7

ETHAN · JANUARY 2017

I stared at the ceiling fan and followed it with my eyes as it went around, and around, and around. Something about being back in a bedroom I grew up in always gave me insomnia. The only thing that was different this time was that I wasn't laying in the bed alone. I looked over and Sloane was fast asleep, with her back facing me.

When I was younger and spent holidays here, I didn't expect the traditions to carry into adulthood. I thought that one day my parents would come back, and we'd be a family again. I only gave up on that hope a few years ago. As much as I hated to admit it, this house was as much mine as it was Graham's. I'd officially reached the age where I lived more of my life as a part of his family than my own.

I carefully slid out of bed, making sure not to wake Sloane in the process. As I entered the hallway, I stopped to look at the wall of photos that I usually tried my hardest to avoid. One that caught my eye particularly was Graham and I on the morning of our high school graduation. At first glance, we looked like a totally normal family. You'd never suspect that was the worst day of my life, so far. I spent it hoping that my mom would show up to the ceremony. She never did. I had to hide how much it hurt as I went to dinner with the Clarks and then got the most wasted that I'd ever been at our friend's graduation party. I slept in a bush in front of the house until noon, when Graham finally found me.

Passing the rest of the memories I'd tried so hard to forget, I went into the kitchen and poured myself another glass of whiskey and opened the sliding doors that led to the back porch. I took a seat in one of the large rocking chairs and reached for the remote that started the fireplace. As I looked out into the vast, snowy mountains, I wondered what my future would look like. This house wasn't really mine, as much as it sometimes felt like it was. My kids wouldn't have grandparents— not biological ones anyway. What kind of dad would I be? Would I be the kind that played football in the front yard? Taught them how to ride a bike? Maybe I wouldn't even have kids. I tried to turn off my thoughts and drown them in whiskey when I heard someone approach from behind me.

"Hey," Sloane said. "Are you okay?"

I didn't want her here. Not to be a dick, but I'd never leaned on anyone my entire life, so why would I start? She couldn't fix me so why was she trying?

"I just needed some space," I answered.

"From me?"

I struggled to explain to her how I felt, but I tried. She didn't pity me, she just tried to understand. I appreciated that. I'd known for a while that she was falling in love with me— it was written all over her face and melted into every interaction I had with her. I felt bad knowing that I'd never be able to love her the same way she loved me. It's not that I didn't want to, a big part of me did. I just knew I couldn't. I also knew that stringing her along wasn't fair. I knew what I needed to do.

Chapter 8

I got back from class to find Ethan waiting outside of my apartment, which put an instant smile on my face. For a quick second, I imagined what it would be like coming home to him every day. He made the bad days better. I'd like to think I'd never have another bad day if each day started and ended with him.

"Get dressed, we're leaving 20," Ethan said as he followed me into my bedroom and made himself comfortable on the bed while I touched up my hair and makeup.

He pressed his foot to the gas and my Honda Civic accelerated down College Road. I watched as he sang along to the radio while his hand rested on my thigh. A little over six months ago was the first time I'd ever laid eyes on him. Before him, I was afraid I'd never meet the right person. I wanted so badly to believe what people said about soulmates— that one day you meet someone who everyone would fall into place with, and you realize why it never worked out with anyone else. I'd like to think that someone for me was Ethan.

He wiggled his hand into a rip in my jeans and looked over at me from the driver's seat like he wanted to have me right then and there.

"Stop it!" I laughed.

"Come on, not even a quickie? I can find somewhere to pull over," he pleaded.

"I thought this was supposed to be my surprise birthday dinner," I argued.

"You know I'm always hungrier after sex." He winked.

"Key word: *my* birthday dinner."

He turned his attention back to the road. My least favorite love language was physical touch and that was Ethan's preferred method of communication. It wasn't that I didn't enjoy it, but the way he'd touch me sometimes felt like he only wanted me for one thing—sex. Even though I knew our relationship was deeper than physical intimacy, it was still a thought that lingered in the back of my mind often.

The car pulled into an Outback parking lot, which wasn't a terrible restaurant choice for a college student on a budget. Ethan ordered a bottle of Pinot Noir and even though I preferred Cab, I learned to like it because it was his favorite.

"So, why don't I know when your birthday is?" I asked as the waiter brought over our bottle and two glasses.

"It's in July," he started. "I don't like to celebrate it though."

For the rest of dinner, I didn't ask any more questions about his past or even him in general. I knew it was one of his least favorite subjects and I didn't want the night to go south.

When we got back to the apartment, it was dark and quiet. As I approached the end of the hall that connected our entryway to the kitchen, I turned on the lights and was shocked at the scene in front of me,

"Surprise!" a sea of my closest friends stood in front of me. "Happy birthday, Sloane!"

I turned around and glared at Ethan, who was still only halfway down the hall as if he were avoiding being a part of the grand entrance. I wasn't turning 22 until the following week, but Lauren always made a huge deal out of birthdays so knowing her we'd celebrate every day until the real thing.

"I put an outfit on your bed. The bodysuit and skirt you were eyeing at Vestique a few weeks ago!" Lauren whispered.

Sometimes I wondered if she could read my mind or if we were just that in tune. I squeezed her and excused myself so that I could change.

We went downtown to Front Street instead of the usual beach bars. It was unusually warm for a February night, so we took full advantage of the weather and spent the next few hours on the back patio at Husk, buying rounds of green tea shots and requesting throwbacks from the DJ.

"Onto the next!" Graham motioned for us to all chug so we could make our way to the next bar.

I wanted to feel remotely excited about going to Reel for late-night karaoke, but I didn't. Ethan had barely said two words to me since we got out of the Uber which only made me more anxious and less fun. Two things you shouldn't feel on your birthday. I drank my vodka soda too quickly as I listened to Lauren blabber on and on about how Graham invited her on his family trip to Key West this summer. They hadn't even been dating six months and were already planning vacations together; meanwhile most days I wondered if Ethan felt the same way about me as I did about him.

I watched from behind him in line as he talked and laughed with his friends, wishing he would motion for me to come to stand with him and put his arm around me. I would do anything for him to give me just the slightest bit of attention. The bouncer scanned my ID and fastened a wristband around my wrist before telling me to have a good night. When I found our group, Ethan was waiting with a shot and a drink for me.

"What is it?" I asked, referring to the shot.

"Cheers." He winked and lifted his glass up to mine, ignoring the question.

We took our shots simultaneously and immediately I could feel the cheap vodka coming back up. I quickly ran to the bathroom and for the next half hour, I didn't leave the handicapped stall which I'm sure the groups of girls in line were thrilled about.

"Sloane, it's me." Lauren banged on the bathroom door. I wiped my mouth before flushing the toilet and collecting myself.

"Let's go home," I said as I opened the stall.

"Graham is in a car out front." She led me through the crowd and out of the bar.

"Where's Ethan?" I asked when she opened the car door and the only people inside were the driver and Graham.

"He didn't want to leave," she replied. I could sense the disappointment in her tone of voice. She didn't want to upset me, but she wasn't surprised by his actions.

When we got back to the apartment, I thanked them for taking me home and went straight to my room. I managed to wash my face and put on an oversized t-shirt before getting in bed. The room felt like it was rotating, and the taste of vodka stung the back of my throat. I rolled out of bed and managed to make it to the toilet where I let it all out. Again.

~

The next morning my mouth tasted like a mixture of sour liquor and stale cardboard. A part of me was glad I woke up to an empty bed with the way my breath probably smelt. Mostly though, I was gutted. My hand smacked my nightstand a few times before locating my phone. My thumb hit the home button and the brightness was overwhelming.

Ethan Brady: 2 Missed Calls

I checked the clock before calling him back, it read 11 am. He was awake, right? I can't believe I'd slept this late. I could feel my body tensing up as the phone rang. Once, twice.

"Hey," he picked up on the third ring.

"You called?" I answered in an irritated tone.

"I'm sorry I didn't leave with you last night. I just wasn't ready to go yet."

"Yeah, Graham told me. It was shitty of you."

"I know and I'm sorry."

We sat in silence for a minute or two, neither of us knowing what to say.

"What're we doing here, Ethan?"

"I don't know, Sloane."

More silence.

"I know I said I didn't want a relationship at first, but I feel like things have escalated. At least for me they have. I can't keep doing this when I don't know how you feel about me," I said as I rubbed my temples, my head pounding from the massive hangover.

"Obviously I like you," he started. "I just need to think about things. Is that okay?"

"Yeah, I'm gonna go back to sleep. My head's killing me."

"I'll text you later. Feel better."

And just like that, the conversation was over. I got a half-assed apology and still had no idea where we stood. I groaned in agony of hangover and heartbreak, maybe that was dramatic, and pulled the covers over my head.

When I finally decided I was ready to wake up for the day, it was nearly time to eat dinner. I checked my phone, expecting to find messages from Ethan and Lauren but frowned when I had no new notifications. I dragged myself into the bathroom and blasted Taylor Swift on shuffle to put myself in a better mood. There was nothing that a hot shower and "All Too Well" couldn't fix. By the time I got out of the shower, I heard Jordan and Lauren in the kitchen, so I threw on some clothes and joined them.

"Wow, we thought you were dead." Jordan laughed.

"Very funny." I glared as I filled up my water bottle from the Brita.

"So, the elephant in the room..." Lauren broke the ice. "Have you heard from Ethan?"

"We talked on the phone earlier. It didn't help though; I think it might've made me more confused. This whole situation is just— *ugh*. This is exactly what I didn't want to happen." I shook my head.

"Like it or not, it's happening, babe. Seems like you and Ethan need to DTR."

"DTR?" Jordan asked.

"Define the relationship," I explained. "Yeah, I know, I know. Can we end this conversation before my head explodes and get some food?"

~

I was spiraling. I hadn't heard from Ethan in almost three days, even after trying to stage multiple parking lot and stairwell run ins. After we got off the phone on Saturday morning, I waited around for a text from him— it never came, and I was too stubborn to send one first. So, we just hadn't spoken.

Jordan dragged me to a Sigma Chi party that night and then we went on a boat with a few of her high school friends the next day. Then, it was Monday, and I was forced to face the reality of what was happening— Ethan was ghosting me. Just as I was picking up my phone to text Ethan, a message from him popped up on my screen.

Ethan Brady: Sorry I've been MIA. Just needed space to think about things. Can we talk in my car?

He was ending it before it even had a chance to begin. My hands started to shake as I replied with one word.

Me: Sure.

A few minutes later, I walked outside to the parking lot and saw his headlights on. He was waiting for me. Rain droplets started to fall from the sky and I knew that couldn't be a good sign. I swallowed as I opened the passenger side door and got into the car, anxious for what was to come. Conversations in cars were never a good thing.

"Hey." The tone in his voice was different.

"Hi."

"I don't know how to say this," he started, and I could feel knots forming in my stomach. "Things between us escalated so fast and became something I can't, and don't, do. I shouldn't have let it get this far but I think we should stop hanging out."

My bottom lip quivered, and I tried to pull myself together before responding.

"Do you, I mean, did you not have feelings for me?"

"I do. Which is why I can't let this go any further. I'm never going to give you what you want."

"Which is what, exactly?" I attested.

"A relationship. I'm not that guy and I'll never be that guy. I would just wind up hurting you even more than I already have."

The words stung.

"I, we, don't have to date. I told you I wasn't sure if I wanted that either." I tried to lie to him and myself, knowing I was way past that point. "I'm happy right now, really."

"Sloane, it's not that. It's that eventually, this is going to have to be something more. That's always how it goes."

"Always how it goes?"

"I just mean, we both have feelings for each other we can't just continue doing whatever this is forever." He motions at himself and then to me. "The longer we do this, the worse it's going to hurt in the end."

"Why is it such a bad thing for you to like someone? I don't get it. Am I not enough?"

His face drops. "Don't think for a second that any of this is your fault. It's not at all. You're too good for me. I don't deserve this. I don't want to take you down with me."

We sat side by side as the rain pounded his windshield and my heart pounded in my chest. I couldn't look at him. I grabbed the door handle, stepped out of the car and let the sky completely soak me as I headed back to the apartment.

Luckily Lauren and Jordan weren't home, so I locked my bedroom door and buried myself underneath the covers. I couldn't even bother to change out of my wet clothes, that's how emotionally drained I was. I silently cried myself to sleep.

I'd never hurt like that before. How was I so easily able to fall in love with someone who wasn't sure about me? He would rather leave than try and that spoke volumes.

Chapter 9

ETHAN · FEBRUARY 2017

No part of me wanted to hurt Sloane. The day we met I knew things would be different with her, which is why I tried to stay away. I wasn't looking for a relationship but something about her made me want to try. It just wasn't enough. I realized that eventually I was going to end up hurting her one way or another— even more than I already had. Seeing her cry last night made me want to tell her everything. I wanted to lay it all out for her so she would understand, but I couldn't. I didn't want to be this way but it's who I was after a life of heartbreak and disappointment.

I unplugged my phone from the charger and scrolled aimlessly for a little while. My thumb wavered over the Facebook app icon before I decided to tap it. In the search bar, her name was recently viewed. I clicked on her latest profile picture, which said it was posted two weeks ago. The Christmas tree in the background told me the photo was taken around the holidays. She was smiling and posing with her daughter. My half-sister.

I closed out of the app before I spiraled down that rabbit hole any further and rolled over. As much as I hated to admit it, I missed Sloane. I missed the comfort of sharing a bed with her every night. Knowing she was next to me made it easier to sleep.

Wow, that was something I never thought I'd say.

~

The next morning, I wandered out of bed and into the kitchen where Graham was making a huge stack of protein pancakes while Jake played video games. In the two years we'd been roommates, absolutely nothing had changed.

"Hey man, want some?" Graham motioned toward the plate of food.

"No bacon?" I asked as I took a seat at the counter.

"In the oven. I'm too lazy to deal with a mess this morning," he replied. "So, were you gonna tell me about Sloane?"

"Shit. It's barely been 12 hours since our conversation. News travels fast around Ascent. Lauren, I assume?"

"Yep. So, what happened?"

I turned around to see if Jake paused the game to hop into the conversation, but he still had his headset on which meant I could be a little more honest. I didn't mind talking about things with Jake; there's just a lot he doesn't know about me that I don't want to have to explain.

"I didn't want to string her along anymore. It's not fair."

"Well yeah, we all knew that. I thought you liked her. At least it seemed like it." Graham pulled the tray full of bacon out of the oven and set it on the stove.

"It's not that simple," I said. "I'm not ready for a full-on relationship. Do I have fun with her? Yes. Do I like her? Yes. Do I want the responsibilities and expectations that come with a relationship? No. That's what made me realize I needed to end things before they got too deep."

"Seems like you were a little too late, buddy." He handed me the plate of bacon and I took a handful before Jake devoured the rest.

"What time should we hit the gym today?" Jake asked.

"I have class until four, do you want to meet then?" Graham replied.

"Works for me. I'll be in the library until then if anyone wants to stop by in between classes today. 3rd floor." I shoved a piece of bacon in my mouth and patted Graham on the back as a thank you before going into my room to shower and head to campus. Sloane's class schedule was nearly impossible to keep track of, so I decided it was probably best to hide out in the library most of the day to avoid any run ins. I didn't want to upset her more than I already had.

Chapter 10

SLOANE · MARCH 2017

One month without contact and I was becoming a different person. Winter had slowly turned into spring and the extra freckles I got from the sun were starting to come out again. I had stories Ethan had never heard and memories he wasn't present for. One month without contact and I was finally starting to feel okay again.

Lauren was dragging me to Pike's formal. Last week I'd put up a fight because I wasn't sure that I was ready to see Ethan yet, but I realized I had to stop putting my life on pause for someone who was no longer a part of it. Usually formal was a whole weekend down in Savannah, but since the chapter was on probation, fraternity standards required them to host an event monitored by the university.

"Think of it this way— running into him at formal is better than running into him at a bar. Here you'll have a date to distract you. Plus, Reese is hot. That never hurts." Lauren winked.

"Fine, you're right, I guess. Which shoes?" I held up

two pairs of heels.

"Black. You can never go wrong with an all-black moment."

"Ladies, you ready?" Graham knocked before entering.

We took a group tequila shot before heading to the bus pickup lot. The closer we got to campus, the more uneasy I started to feel. All I needed to do was make sure I didn't throw up or cry when I saw Ethan. Simple enough.

When the pledge driver pulled up, the parking lot was already full of people. Luckily, no sign of Ethan as far as I could tell. My stomach started to feel uneasy, but I did my best to hold it together.

"Let's find Reese," Graham said. "Sloane, you've met him before, right?"

"Once or twice at a party, I think," I replied.

"He's cool. Good guy," he assured me.

"Reese!" Lauren waved him down.

Reese was tall, well over 6 feet. He had short hair that was dirty blonde, and I could tell he had recently shaved, though he didn't look like the type that grew much facial hair. When Graham gave me the low down on Reese, I learned he should've graduated last year but had to stay for an extra semester after he missed a few credits.

"You made it!" Reese reached out to side hug me. "Ready to get wasted?"

"Am I ever." Lauren grabbed a water bottle full of vodka from Graham's back pocket and passed it around.

I scanned the crowd one more time for any sign of Ethan before we piled into the party bus. Maybe he wasn't coming after all. I felt myself begin to relax and start to try and enjoy the night. It was a little over a forty-minute ride to the venue but thankfully we brought plenty of roadies. I took a seat halfway through the drive and by the time I stood up to get off the bus I could feel the Smirnoff rush through my entire body. Vodka was never my friend.

"Woah there." Reese grabbed my arm and helped me balance. "I've got you. Let's go inside." He took my hand and guided me off the bus, which I was thankful for because I wasn't sure I could feel my legs.

"This is a really nice place," I observed.

I expected the restaurant to be a slight step up from our usual dive bars but was surprised to see white tablecloths, a live band, and a buffet with chicken tenders and mozzarella sticks. It reminded me of a low budget wedding planned by a former fraternity event chair. Reese gripped my hand tightly and led me to the bar where a huge line had already formed. I wrapped my hands around his forearm to keep my balance. From the back of the crowd, I could see Lauren and Graham had almost made their way to the front.

"Should we cut the line?" I asked.

"It'll move fast, they have four bartenders," he said. "Are you ready for graduation?"

"Yeah, I guess," I replied. "I'm still not sure what I'm doing."

"It'll happen, you still have plenty of time. I'm moving to New York right after finals." Reese was trying to make conversation with me in the middle of the loud and crowded bar. I couldn't tell if it was because he was interested in me, wanted to sleep with me, or was just being nice. Either way, I played along.

"Oh yeah, I think Graham mentioned that. I love New York. It's always been a dream of mine to move there and become a writer."

"What kind of writer?"

"I don't know. I just love to write." I shrugged.

"Well, if you do end up in the city, I'm sure you'll love it. I've interned there every summer since freshman year and never want to leave. Well, once I move there in August, anyway. I finally got offered a full-time role when I left this past summer."

I listened to Reese as he told me about his new boss, the apartment he and a friend from high school just signed a lease for, and his favorite spots there to go out after work. As we got closer to the front of the line, I became less and less interested in what he had to say. I looked across the bar to see if there was a drink menu or specials. I reached over to the girl next to me to grab a laminated card from under someone's hand, accidentally brushing it.

"Can I see this?" I said, looking up at whoever's hand was resting on the cocktail menu.

Our eyes met and my stomach dropped.

"Oh, sorry," I quickly replied.

"All good, you can have it." Ethan lifted his arm off the bar, and I watched his eyes glance over to Reese. I grabbed the menu and quickly turned back around.

"What do you want?" Reese asked.

"Double vodka soda with lime. Let's do shots too."

"Two tequila shots and two double vodka sodas," he ordered.

I tried to enjoy the night with Reese, even though when my incoherent mind could form thoughts. The only thing I could think about was Ethan.

~

Like most mornings when I drank, I could taste stale alcohol on my tongue. I managed to open my eyes to the sight of grey striped bedsheets and a Carolina Panthers poster on the wall adjacent to me. Whoever's bedroom I was in, I wasn't familiar with it.

I turned over and there was Reese. Laying on his back, breathing so heavily it could've been confused with light snoring. I inched my way out of the covers and down to the foot of the bed without waking him. His bathroom was surprisingly clean for a 23-year-old guy, but the toilet paper roll was empty. I searched around for a second before I decided to just drip dry. Quietly, I made my way out of the bathroom and searched Reese's room for any sign of my phone or purse.

"Morning," he said groggily. "Do want me to take you home?"

Shit. I woke him up.

"It's okay. Once I find my phone, I can call an Uber or Lauren."

"Your stuff is on the coffee table. You fell asleep on the couch last night and I put you back here. I offered to take the couch, but you told me to sleep here. I'm not sure how much you remember…" He trailed off.

"No, totally, I remember," I lied. "Thanks so much. Sorry that I got so drunk, I shouldn't have pre-gamed so hard."

"Seriously, just let me drive you." He got out of bed in just a pair of boxers. His body was more toned than I expected.

"Here." I handed him a t-shirt that was hanging on the back of his desk chair. "I'll grab my stuff and wait out there."

The car ride home was silent.

"This is me." I pointed to building #3.

"Would you want to get dinner sometime this week?" he asked.

"Oh, um," I stuttered.

"Why don't you put your number in here and you can just think about it?" He handed me his phone. I did as he asked and placed his phone back in the cup holder.

"Thanks again for driving me."

"No problem."

I got out of his car and headed towards the stairs without looking back. I made it into the apartment without running into Ethan, which I'd consider a win.

"Oh my god, finally!" Lauren jumped off the couch.

"Yeah, Sloane, where have you been?" Jordan seemed concerned for once.

"I was wasted. Reese took me back to his place so I could sleep."

"So, you guys didn't hook up?" Lauren asked.

"Do you like him?" Jordan followed.

"I mean, he's nice and I'm attracted to him," I started. "I'm just not sure I'm ready yet. You know?"

I sat next to Lauren and put my head on her shoulder, hoping they'd understand. As much as I wanted to be over Ethan and move on, I just wasn't ready yet.

"Yeah, Lauren said that Ethan was asking about you," Jordan started.

"Jordan, shut up!"

"What did he ask? Why weren't you going to tell me?" I questioned her.

"You've been doing so well. I didn't want his jealousy to set you back. It was just the fact that he saw you there with someone else while he didn't bring a date," she explained.

"He didn't bring a date?" I lit up inside.

"Whatever. Yes, Ethan was there alone. Don't let that give you any kind of false hope though."

While I was relieved, I couldn't help but feel a little angry with myself. I didn't want him to think that I was moving on that quickly or even at all. I just wanted him back.

"I'm going to charge my phone and shower," I announced.

"We're going to get bagels. Want your usual?" Jordan offered.

"Definitely."

I plugged my phone into the charger on my nightstand and headed for my ultimate hangover cure: an ice-cold shower. After those ten minutes of torture were over, I made my way into bed in my robe with a towel on my head and checked my phone.

Lauren: 7 missed calls
Lauren: Did you leave??
Lauren: Where are you?!
Ethan: Hey
Unknown: Hey, it's Reese!

Seeing his name in my inbox felt comfortable, like life was back to normal again though I knew it wasn't. I knew the right thing to do was leave Ethan on read and go on that date with Reese. Why is it always so hard to do the right thing? I wrote back to Ethan and left Reese unanswered for now. When it came to Ethan I had absolutely no self-control, and the sad part was, I think he knew that.

~

An hour later, we were sitting in his car— the same place he broke my heart only a few weeks ago.

"Sorry to do this here, again," Ethan said.

"It's okay."

"I guess I'll just go for it. This thing between us scares me. I don't know how to deal with it. I thought that ending things with you was the right thing to do, for both of us. But when I saw you with someone else…" He paused. "I realized I didn't want that. I know you deserve more than what I can give you, but I owe it to us to at least try."

Relief washed over me, and a smile emerged on my face.

"I still need to take things slow. No title yet, okay? I'm not saying we won't get there; I just don't think we need to rush into it."

I didn't care that I was settling for a fraction of a relationship with him when I knew I deserved so much more. I was willing to settle for whatever he would give me because a fraction of him was better than nothing at all.

I walked back into the apartment dreading having to explain where I was. It's not that the girls didn't like Ethan; it's that they didn't like what he was doing to me. Stringing me along is what they liked to call it. They didn't know him the way I did though. I knew that he wanted to try, he just said it himself. I could tell that he was scared that he'd fail, or he wouldn't live up to my standards. What he didn't see was that I was falling in love with him because I'd been trying to mask it. I was afraid to tell him because once I did, it would be game over. That was the only move I had left, and I wanted to keep it in my back pocket.

"Where'd you just go?" Lauren was sitting at the counter doing schoolwork.

"Ethan and I talked," I said sheepishly.

"Sloane!" Jordan inserted herself into the conversation without moving from the couch. "We just talked about this!"

"He texted me a few times last night and I didn't see them until earlier because my phone was dead. I just wanted to hear what he had to say."

"And what did he have to say?" Lauren asked.

"A lot, but the SparkNotes are that he wants to try again. I feel bad for him. I know this is all new to him, and me I guess, and I feel like I put a lot of pressure on us. We're going to take it slow and try to work up to a relationship."

"Sloane, in the nicest way, do you hear yourself? A relationship isn't supposed to be this hard. Sure, every couple has arguments and makes compromises but the lead-up shouldn't be this long. You've been doing this with him for almost a year now. He should know what he wants."

I fell silent.

"Babe," she continued. "Stop losing your mind over someone who doesn't mind losing you."

I knew she was trying to be sincere, but those words cut deep. While I'd never been one to get angry with Lauren, that instance was the closest I had ever come.

"He does know what he wants; he just doesn't know how to give it to me."

"And that's any better? Why him? What's so special about Ethan?"

"I don't know. I wish I could put it into words. I think he's my first love, which sounds weird because I'm 22. For a while I thought I loved Carter, I mean I kept an entire journal about it. But the more I think about it, what I had with him wasn't love; it was an attachment. He was just a distraction when I needed it the most."

"I can see that," Lauren nodded.

"This thing with Ethan is different though," I continued. "Right off the bat, I knew there was chemistry between us and then it started to grow into this confusing, but sort of beautiful, connection. He's the first person that I've ever been this close to, and I know that's not saying much, but to me it's something."

"I just want you to be happy and if he makes you happy, then I'm all for it."

Chapter 11

ETHAN · MARCH 2017

I spotted Sloane across the room as soon as I entered the venue. She was wearing a tight black dress and her long, auburn hair was pulled back, which was unusual for her. She looked beautiful, though. After I was done admiring her, I realized that she wasn't alone.

Seeing her with someone else made my stomach turn in a way I never knew possible. One of my fraternity brothers though? That stung more than it should have. I couldn't blame her for moving on when I was the one who drove her away, but I didn't expect for it to happen that fast. Maybe I didn't want it to happen at all. Was I wrong for feeling that way?

I snuck up to the bar, hoping to grab a drink and avoid running into her. As I waited for the bartender to return with my whiskey soda, Sloane appeared next to me but seemed to not realize I was standing next to her. I was praying that the bartender would hurry up so it could stay that way, but of course it didn't.

"Can I see this?" she asked without looking up.

I removed my resting arm off the cocktail menu and then our eyes met.

"Oh, sorry," she quickly replied.

"All good, you can have it." The bartender returned with my drink, and I quickly escaped into the crowd to find Graham. I found him on the edge of the dance floor, attached at Lauren's hip. He waved me down and I reluctantly went over, knowing that Sloane would be at the bar for at least a little while longer.

"Hey dude," Graham greeted me. "I thought you had work?"

"Got off early, so I figured I'd stop by. You didn't mention Sloane was Reese's date."

"And for good reason."

Was Graham really taking Sloane's side on this? Not that he needed to take a side, necessarily. I just thought we could be adults about all this considering we weren't even dating. I scanned the room until I saw Jake talking with a group of brothers. I joined in on the conversation and stayed far away from Sloane and Reese for the rest of the night.

~

I could barely sleep. When I got home, I had sent Sloane a text, hoping that she'd reply and maybe somehow find her way into my bed. But when I woke up, there were no new messages from Sloane. I rolled over and decided since I had nothing productive to do, sleeping and avoiding my problems would be best. It was around 2 p.m. when I finally received a response from her.

Fifteen minutes later, she was walking up to my passenger side door. I fidgeted with my phone while I waited for her to get into the car. I wasn't sure that I was ready to do what I was about to, but I knew I didn't like how it felt to see her with someone else. So, I had to do something. Right?

During our conversation, I made promises to Sloane that I wasn't sure I could keep. Maybe somewhere, deep down, I knew it was better to let her go but I really wanted to be the person she needed me to be. I felt like I at least owed it to her to try.

Chapter 12

I wanted to feel even remotely excited about graduation, about interviewing for jobs and touring apartments in new cities— but the truth is I was dreading all of it. Even though Ethan and I hadn't put a label on things, the thought of moving away from him made my stomach churn. I tried my hardest not to think about it, but that was hard considering both Lauren and my mom nagged me daily about finding a job.

"Oh my God, oh my God!" Lauren screamed as I ran down the hall with Jordan practically at my heels.

"What?"

"I got a teaching job in New York!" she said. "I just received the offer letter!"

"Holy shit, Laur, that's huge!" I congratulated her.

"We're halfway there!" she squealed. "Now it's your turn, then we can start apartment hunting."

While I was so happy for Lauren, I couldn't help but feel defeated that I hadn't heard back from any of the dozens of places I'd applied to.

"Jordan, are you sure you don't want to try being a city girl? Just for a year?" Lauren pouted.

"Let's face it, I'm never leaving Wilmington." Jordan laughed. "And marketing coordinator at the yacht club really isn't a bad gig. Think about it— hot guys, hot rich guys, hot rich guys with boats…"

"Okay, okay don't make me jealous." Lauren laughed. "I'm going to call my parents before I sign this. Love you guys so much!"

She squeezed us into a group hug before shooing us out of her room. For the rest of the day, I searched high and low for any job in New York that matched my resume. By the time my laptop was at 5% battery I had applied to dozens of positions and decided that was enough. I shut my computer and pulled out my phone to finally reply to a few missed texts.

Ethan Brady: Heyo, how's your day?

Me: Could be better. Just applied to what felt like a hundred jobs. Lauren got one today and I'm worried I won't :(

Ethan Brady: Stop saying that. You're so smart and talented. You're gonna get something, I just know it. And don't settle either.

Me: Ugh, it's just exhausting. I should've started applying months ago.

Ethan Brady: Stop being so hard on yourself. Seriously, Hart. Be less hard than I am every time you walk into a room ;)

Me: You're the worst.

Ethan Brady: You like it. Night Hart.

Me: Goodnight ;)

~

The next day, Lauren signed her teaching contract and broke up with Graham. It was like she didn't even flinch. The two of us got lunch on campus while she ran me through it play-by-play.

"I don't get it," I said. "Why wouldn't you try long distance?"

"Sloane, it's simple," she said, shoving a waffle fry into her mouth. "Graham's a good guy, but he's not the one. I'm only 22; I want to move to the city as a free woman and have no regrets. I'm not ready to settle down. I jumped into things with Graham so soon because they were easy and honestly, I liked his company. But now, I'm ready to be on my own."

Sometimes I wondered how Lauren was wise beyond her years. There I was, pining over a guy I wasn't even dating and afraid to leave his side, while Lauren just broke up with a good guy because she didn't want to be tied down. I wished that I had her confidence and sense of security. Even in the most unsure moments, she always seemed to know what she was doing.

"Well, how did he take it then?" I sipped my Dr. Pepper.

"He, uh, cried." I could tell she felt bad. "But hopefully we can move past this and be friends one day. Especially if you and Ethan stay together."

If. I hated hearing that word, but I knew she was right. *If* we stayed together. The odds were slim, but I was taking my chances. When it came to Ethan, I was all in.

~

That weekend, after I asked Ethan if Graham would be okay with it, Jordan and I convinced Lauren to go to

Pike's LDOC party. It was a tradition we couldn't miss, and I was glad Graham could put aside his feelings and let us have one final night together, as neighbors and friends.

We walked into the split-level house that was covered in any decorations you'd need for a luau. Blow up palm trees stood in every corner, lanterns hung from the ceiling and leis were around the banister for people to grab as they walked in. Girls were dressed in bikini tops and cut off shorts, guys in swim trunks and tank tops. Somehow, they had even managed to cover the dining room in sand. I felt bad for whatever brothers had to clean that up in the morning.

I spotted Ethan almost immediately and waved to him and Graham. We agreed not to pre-game together and as much as I hated the idea of being apart from Ethan at first, it was a really special way to close out college with the girls that got me through it.

"Come on." I grabbed Lauren and Jordan by the arm and led them into living room.

"Sloaney bologna!" Graham picked me up and spun me around. I could tell he was already wasted based on the new nickname he'd just given me.

"Put me down!" I demanded.

"Okay, okay," he listened. "Ladies, what'll you have to drink?"

"PJ works," Lauren replied. "Thanks Graham."

He half smiled at her and disappeared into the kitchen.

"Well, that wasn't too bad," Ethan whispered.

"I can hear you, you know," Lauren pointed out.

"Let's dance!" Jordan dragged Lauren to the basement, and I reluctantly followed, leaving Ethan to entertain Graham.

By 1 a.m. the kegs were kicked and the coolers full of PJ were dry. I scanned the basement full of sweaty twenty-something-year-olds until I located Ethan near the bar with Jake.

"Should we call an Uber?" Lauren asked.

Before I replied, I looked over to Ethan again. I wanted to stay there with him, instead of babysit Lauren but I knew if roles were reversed, she would do it for me.

"Yeah, can you?" I handed her my phone. "I'm gonna go say bye to Ethan." As I walked in his direction, I watched his eyes take me in.

"Hey," he said. "Are you leaving?"

"Yeah, I'm gonna get Lauren home."

"Where's Jordan?" Ethan looked around the room.

"She left to go to another party an hour or so ago."

"Why don't I get a sober brother to take you guys? You can make sure she gets home okay and then he'll drive you back to the house."

"You're sure?" I asked.

"Yeah, we're gonna post-game and I don't want you to go home yet," he reassured me.

Then, he kissed me. I felt on top of the world.

A freshman drove us back to Ascent and waited in the parking lot until we saw Lauren reach the second floor. She waved to us, and he started driving back in the direction of the post-game.

"So, you're Brady's girlfriend?" he asked.

"I wouldn't say that," I replied. "I mean, I don't know."

I never knew how to describe us. Technically, we weren't dating but we were exclusive. At least, that's what

I thought. I hated how a title held our entire relationship in its hands. To me, we were very much in love. The most in love I've ever been. But to him? Well, I didn't really know how he felt. All I knew was what his body language told me and what I felt. I knew he loved me. Deep down, I knew. Even if he hadn't told me yet. He didn't have to say it out loud for me to know how he felt. That was the best part about us.

"That's cool," he replied.

This guy probably wouldn't even remember this conversation when he woke up in the morning, yet the question he asked would loom over me for days, maybe even weeks.

I got out of the car and thanked him for the ride. I couldn't wait to see Ethan again. Walking into the fraternity house alone was always so nerve-wracking. I entered through the front door and walked through the foyer to find the guys settled into all the old leather couches in the living room.

"Sup, Sloane," one of them greeted me.

"There she is!" Graham echoed.

I took a seat next to Ethan and he squeezed my thigh. I was so glad I came back. I loved how it felt when he showed me the slightest bit of attention.

The boys passed around slices of pizza that they ordered once the party died down. They offered me some, but I declined. I hated eating in front of people, especially when I drank.

"Let's go home," Ethan whispered in my ear. *Home.*

Brothers had stopped driving once everyone from the party got home, so Ethan called an Uber and I shuffled into the back seat behind him. He pulled me so close to him that I was almost sitting on top of him. He kissed me and his breath tasted like whiskey. Fireball, to be specific. I relished it. I parted my mouth to let him in and I let the happiness flood in too. We got dropped off in the parking lot and he held my hand up the entire three flights of stairs to his apartment.

As I opened the refrigerator and reached for the Brita, Ethan pulled the yanked the string on the back of my bikini top and it fell to the ground.

"Ethan!" I gasped and covered myself.

"No one's home." He smirked. "Let's do it here."

"In the kitchen? What if Graham or Jake walks in—"

He put a finger over my mouth, picked me up and set me on the granite countertop. With the force of his lower body, he spread open my legs and stood between them. His mouth came so close to mine, that I could smell the Fireball again, but he wouldn't let me taste it yet. His hands found their way to the button on my denim mini skirt, while his lips were on my neck. He picked me up off the counter while managing to wiggle my skirt and my underwear off me so that I was completely naked and sitting on his kitchen counter. Within seconds his swimsuit was on the floor, and he was inside of me.

I wasn't one for spontaneous sex that anyone could've walked in on at any moment, but for Ethan, I'd do almost anything.

~

The next morning the hangover was enough to swear off PJ, and vodka, for the rest of my life. I guess it was a good thing that yesterday was my last day of undergrad.

"Finally." Ethan's voice made my head pound even harder. "Your phone's been going off for like twenty minutes."

I snatched the phone off the nightstand and sat up as fast as I could without getting too lightheaded. When I unlocked it, I had two missed calls and a voicemail from a 212 area code. Did I even know where that area code was from? I held the phone up to my ear as I played the message.

"Hi Sloane, this is Annie Walker. I'm a senior editor at *The Gist*. I reviewed your application for the staff writer position we have open, and I'd love to talk with you more about it. Today, if possible. Give me a call, I'll be around all day. Thanks!"

Holy shit.

"Holy shit!" I screamed.

Ethan darted back into the room, grasping a bottle of Advil and a glass of ice water. The look on his face told me that he was extremely worried to hear whatever I was about to tell him.

"I have an interview!" I jumped out of his bed. He wrapped his arms around me and I felt the condensation from the glass seep through my shirt.

"That's amazing but you almost just scared the shit out of me." Ethan laughed and handed me two blue tablets. I put them in my mouth, followed by a large gulp of water.

"It's for a company I literally didn't think I'd hear back from. I was applying as a shot in the dark. I can't believe she looked at my application! I need to call her back." I kissed him, grabbed my purse, shoes and clothes from the night before and made my way down a single flight of stairs and into my apartment.

I pressed the callback number for Annie as I shut my bedroom door and paced the room.

"Hi, is this Annie?"

"Hi! Sloane?"

"Yes! I just got your voicemail, sorry for missing your call. It's finals week so life is a little crazy with that and graduation prep."

"Such an exciting time for you! I'm glad you got my message. Would you be able to hop on a quick Skype call sometime today? I'd love to have a casual conversation and get to know you— I know this doesn't give you much time to prepare for a formal interview, but I promise it will be simple."

"Yes, of course, I'd love that! I can do any time after one o'clock today." I glanced at the clock, it was almost 11 a.m. which meant I had plenty of time to shower, look presentable, and do my background research on Annie's career path.

"That's great! Let's plan for two. I'll email over a calendar invite and Skype link."

"Looking forward to it!"

I threw the phone on my bed and started stripping out of my clothes to get ready for a shower. This moment called for an upbeat Taylor Swift playlist. There was no better way to prep for an interview, first date, or anything that made us nervous than the "Hype Taylor Swift" Spotify playlist Lauren and I made freshman year.

I lathered shampoo into my hair and started mentally preparing myself for what would be the biggest interview of my life so far. *The Gist* wasn't just one of the dozens of places in New York that I'd applied to; it was one of my top choices. Though it was only founded a little over ten years ago, it was one of the trendiest news and entertainment companies in the city.

~

Later that week, I had secured my first full-time job as a staff writer for *The Gist*. Which meant in less than a month, I'd be moving to New York with my best friend. It didn't feel real, none of it did. Especially not the part about having to tell Ethan the news.

For as long as I could remember, I wanted to be a writer. It didn't matter that there wasn't much money in it, I knew that I had to make a career out of something that I loved or else I'd never survive decades of a nine-to-five. That passion was writing. I couldn't believe that I had pulled it off. *The Gist* wasn't as well-known as *Cosmopolitan,* but it was a start. It was my start, and it was only up from there.

That afternoon, Ethan and I had plans to get lunch and walk on the beach. I sat in the kitchen perusing apartments on StreetEasy until he came downstairs to let me know he was ready to go. He drove us to my favorite restaurant, Dockside. I loved to sit on the back deck and watch the boats speed by while the sun glistened on the water. It reminded me of summer— which was Wilmington in its best form.

"Should we get fried pickles?" he suggested.

"Yes, and drinks! We're celebrating," I replied.

"Celebrating what?" He raised an eyebrow.

"I got the job!" I beamed.

"I knew you'd get it! I'm so proud of you." My heart skipped a beat hearing him say those five words.

"Thank you." I smiled.

"When do you start? Or I guess, when do you move?" He looked uncomfortable, almost as if it were hard to say those words.

"Could we talk about all of that after lunch? At the beach? I just want to enjoy this for right now and not have a hard conversation," I offered.

"Sure, of course," he replied as he waved down our server to put in for drinks.

Once we finished lunch, Ethan parked his car in a paid parking lot, and we walked over a street to Public Access #25. My stomach started to feel uneasy, and my hands were clamming up. I wasn't ready to have this conversation with him, but we both knew it needed to happen.

"What does this mean for us?" I broke the ice.

"I'm not sure." He shuffled his feet in the sand. We walked in silence for a few minutes before one of us knew what else to say.

"Does it have to mean anything?" I asked.

"No," he replied. "I guess it doesn't."

"So, we can just continue doing what we're doing? Will you visit?"

"I'll visit," he assured me.

~

The night before my one-way flight to New York I slept at Ethan's, though my anxiety kept me from doing any sleeping. For the last year, Ethan had been the biggest comfort for me since my parents in their pre-divorce era. I told him everything and truly felt like he listened and tried to understand me. I was already losing so many things in the move; I didn't want to lose him too. I couldn't lose him.

He held me while I silently cried into his chest. The thought of leaving him behind made me feel miserable. Long distance? We couldn't even have a functional relationship when we lived a hundred feet away from each other. How were we going to make 600 miles work? Deep down, I think I knew it wouldn't last but I decided to hold on anyway.

Chapter 13

SLOANE · JUNE 2017

Our first month as locals in the city went smoother than expected. While she waited for the school year to start, Lauren found a family to nanny for and I quickly settled into my first post-grad job. The apartment we were subletting for six months was further uptown than we'd wanted but it was important for us to figure out our favorite neighborhood before signing a year-long lease. I didn't mind being a little far from work because it gave me a chance to get acquainted with the subway system.

The wheels of the train steamrolled under me as I made my way down into midtown for a half-day at work. After a month of FaceTime dates, I'd finally convinced Ethan to visit, and his flight would get in late afternoon. I expected to miss him, but the hole I felt in my life was much larger than I'd ever anticipated. I've grown to hate it, especially sleeping alone.

The subway came to a halt, and I quickly got off at my usual stop, 5th and 53rd, right across the street from *The Gist* HQ. The building dripped of New York City charm.

It was made of old brick and had a total of forty floors, all with large windows and beautiful Renaissance architecture. I walked a few blocks down to my favorite coffee shop, like I did most mornings, and treated myself to a latte.

When I entered the building, I pressed the button for floor 16 and stared down at the Gucci mules my dad gifted me for graduation. I know he probably spent a lot of his alimony on them, so I wore them almost every day, except on casual Fridays when I rotated through each pair of sneakers in my closet. Every morning when the elevator doors opened to *The Gist* lobby, it reminded me that I achieved a job I'd been dreaming about since I learned how to read. Even though life without Ethan was hard, working there made long distances almost worth it.

"Morning, Kim!" I waved to her as I headed into the main workspace.

Kim was the CEO's executive assistant but doubled as the front desk secretary because she's the biggest people-person at our company. In just a month, Kim had become like a second mom to me.

"Lunch today?" she called out.

"Friday tradition! I'll see what Mila wants and we'll meet you down here after our 11:30 meeting."

Mila and I started on the same day and our cubicles share a wall. She was hired as an associate editor and worked on a lot of my pieces, so we spent a lot of time together.

"You're here!" Mila spun around in her chair as I stood in the doorway of her cube.

"You're early." I laughed.

"I was up at 5 a.m. thanks to a cockroach in my sheets.

I've never gotten out of bed faster. I grabbed breakfast and have been ideating on new topics. Want to meet to go over them before we pitch Monday?"

"Works for me," I replied. "Have you been looking for new places to live?"

"My only other option right now is my parents. We'd have to pay a few grand to break our lease, so I can't afford anything else." She seemed defeated.

The apartment she lived in was on top of a convenience store that always left a ton of trash in the alley. In the past week, her roommates had killed eight cockroaches and trapped two mice.

"I'll get the number of our exterminator for you; I totally forgot to ask Lauren last time."

"Thanks. Is 10 a good time to meet? That gives you two hours to work through the edits I delivered to your inbox."

"Sounds perfect." I put in my headphones and got to work.

~

When I got home, I scanned every inch of the apartment to make sure everything looked as presentable as possible. My mom would be proud.

Since Ethan's Uber got stuck in traffic and the drive from LaGuardia was already a hike, I had enough time to stop into the bodega and liquor store on my way home. I put together a small charcuterie board and poured a glass of whiskey on ice for him and a tequila soda for myself. I hoped that was still his favorite.

"I think he's here!" Lauren shouted.

I ran to her room and joined her in looking out of the window. Ethan was wearing a navy tee shirt and the grey

Lululemon shorts I helped him pick out. His hair was tucked into a baseball cap, but I could tell it had gotten longer by the way it stuck out of the back.

"I'm nervous," I admitted. Butterflies filled my stomach— it felt just like the first time we met.

"Go get him, babe," she nudged me. "I'll join you for a drink and then I'm off to my date."

Lauren downloaded a few dating apps the first week we moved here. Without many friends, the city got lonely very quickly.

I picked up the pace as walked down the stairs of our third-floor walk-up. Through the frosted glass door, I could see Ethan's silhouette. I couldn't believe he was finally here. It didn't feel real.

"Hey, you." His smile filled his entire face as I opened the door to let him in.

"Hi." I smiled back, feeling my face go flush.

The door closed behind him, and he dropped his bag to the floor so he could pull me in for a hug. We stayed like that for a minute before he grabbed my face with both of his hands and stared at me.

"You have more freckles," he noted.

"It's summer."

Then, he kissed me. God, I missed kissing him. I didn't want to go another day without kissing him ever again.

"I've missed you," I said when our lips pulled apart. Instead of replying, Ethan just kissed me again.

"Show me the way, Hart." He picked up his bag and motioned for me to walk ahead of him.

"Lauren's home but she's leaving for a date in a little. Knowing her, they'll be out all night," I joked, sort of.

We walked through the front door, and I watched as

Ethan took in the sight before his eyes. Our apartment wasn't the nicest, but we made it work. It had a large living room and a small kitchen that was the size of a closet. Luckily, we didn't cook much.

"Hey guys, hope you don't mind I poured myself a glass to take the edge off." Lauren stood at our makeshift bar, which was just a tall console table and barstools that backed up to our couch.

"Hey Lauren." Ethan gave her a side hug. "How's the city life treating you?"

"Honestly, the dating scene sucks, but you can't really be too sad about anything when you live in Manhattan. You know?"

"I hear ya. Where's your room?" He looked at me. "I'm gonna shower and change if that's cool."

"Down there to your right. And the bathroom is the door straight ahead between both of our rooms. There's a towel on my dresser for you."

Once Ethan had disappeared down the hallway, I turned to Lauren and shot her a huge smile. I loved that his presence did that to me.

"Alright, stop making me so jealous," she mocked me.

"So, where's the date?" I asked.

"Some bar in the West Village." She shrugged. "I think it's close to his place. I'm not trying to crash with you two tonight."

"Don't feel like you can't come back!" I reassured her.

"I know, I just really don't want to." Lauren laughed. "Okay, I'm out of here. Have fun tonight!"

Once Lauren was gone, I made my way down the hall to find Ethan. The shower wasn't running but the bathroom door was still closed. I knocked lightly and then peeked my head in before he could answer.

"Hey, hey!" He quickly covered himself up.

"Oh shush, can you get ready so we can actually spend time together?" I wrapped my arms around his torso and pressed my cheek up to his back. I didn't care that my clothes were getting wet from spots he didn't fully dry.

"Anything for you." He grabbed my hand and kissed it.

"Seriously." I led him into the bedroom so he could change.

"Is Lauren gone? What if we just—" With one swift move, my body was flush against his bare chest.

"We have a reservation!" I frowned.

"Alright, alright."

~

Summer in Manhattan was surprisingly hot, especially underground. By the time we got off the subway, we were five minutes late for our dinner reservation. The top restaurant to try that summer, according to *The Gist*, was The Smith. We got seated at a two-top in the back of the restaurant, surrounded by other couples. I ordered us an appetizer and a bottle of wine to share.

"I hate to ask but," Ethan started. "Do you mind if we split the check? I had to dip into savings for the plane ticket and I'm not getting as many hours at the golf course as I'd hoped."

"Stop," I cut him off. "I wanted to get tonight's dinner anyway, but we can split everything else this weekend. I'm just glad you're here."

"Thanks." He half smiled.

After we finished our main courses and the bottle of wine, I paid the check and texted Lauren to see where she was so we could meet up. I wasn't ready for the night to end.

"Lauren's at Gem Saloon," I said. "I was thinking we could stop in for a drink?"

"I'm exhausted. Could we just go back to your place and turn on a movie?"

"Sure, yeah, that's fine." I sighed.

"Sloane." He picked up my hand and held it in his. "I just need a breather. Let's pack it all in tomorrow."

When we got back to the apartment, I changed into a big t-shirt and pajama shorts while Ethan poured us each a glass of wine. By the end of the movie, we finished a bottle of red and he was playing with the drawstring on my shorts. A small part of me was mad and didn't want to give into the temptation. I reminded myself how much I'd missed him in the month we spent apart and slid my hand under the waistband of his boxers. I wanted to make him realize how much he missed me and how much he needed me. Maybe then he'd consider moving here.

We made our way to my bedroom, kissing and stumbling the entire way there. I pushed him onto the bed and got on top, both of us still fully dressed. I continued to kiss him and take off his clothes, piece by piece. It turned me on more than anything to know that I was getting him off.

He quickly took control and in one swift motion, he was on top of me.

"Want me to fuck you like I missed you?" he whispered.

The words sent shivers down my spine. For a few minutes, I forgot what it was like to miss him and remembered what it was like to have him.

~

Before my alarm went off, I woke up nestled under Ethan's arm while he laid on his back snoring. Though it may have seemed like a small and insignificant moment, it made me to realize that I wanted to wake up like this every day. After daydreaming about a future with Ethan for a few minutes, I crept out of the room and headed to the bathroom to freshen up. I took a quick glance into Lauren's room to see if she had returned, but her bed was untouched and empty. I quickly got dressed, putting on a sports bra, shorts, and sneakers before heading out to our favorite bagel shop.

When I returned with breakfast, Ethan was laying on the couch in nothing but his boxers, scrolling on his phone. I set the brown bag on the coffee table and handed him a small, hot, black coffee. Just the way he liked it.

"You might want to put some clothes on. Lauren will probably be back soon."

"It's just so hot in here. This window air conditioning unit sucks."

I rolled my eyes. It was like he was trying to hate everything about the city without even giving it a chance. I didn't respond and instead decided to decompress with a shower. Ethan made his way in a few minutes later and I let him because I didn't want to miss another minute with him.

"Why have we never done that before?"

I planted a small kiss on his lips and wrapped the towel around my shivering body. Showering with someone else was one of my least favorite experiences, but I'd never let him know that. I'd do almost anything to please him. I wanted to make him realize that I was more than enough.

"What's on the agenda today?" His mood seemed to have lifted.

"I was thinking we could walk around SoHo and grab lunch. I haven't been down there yet. Then we'll head back here to change before the Yankee game."

"What?"

"I got us tickets to the game tonight. I know it's not a big one, but I got us good seats. I get a discount through work."

"Sloane, that's awesome. Thank you so much." He grabbed my face and kissed it all over. I loved making him happy.

~

It took us over an hour to get into the Bronx. The subway ride was rough, but we brought a water bottle with vodka in it so that made it bearable.

When we got through the line and into Yankee Stadium, we waited in line for two beers and then made our way to section 103.

"These seats are sick!" Ethan said as we sat down.

"You can thank *The Gist*. My salary might be entry level, but the perks we get are great."

"Do they need any new employees?" he joked.

"Very funny. Before the game starts, can we take a picture for my Snapchat story?" I opened the app, pointed the front camera at us and tilted my head closer to his. We both smiled as I snapped the photo.

"Don't post that," he followed it up with.

I took off my sunglasses and looked at him. "Are you serious?"

"You can save it. But just don't post it."

"Why?" I was starting to get pissed off.

"I don't know, I just don't understand why every time girls do something, they have to post about it."

"God forbid you come and visit me in New York, I take you to a Yankee game and want to post about it. I really don't see the big deal. I used to post pictures of us."

"Whatever, just do what you want."

I saved the photo and never posted it. At that point, I didn't want to. Why did he have to be like that? Was he trying to hide that he was visiting me? Was he trying to hide me? The entire game that was all I could think about.

At the bottom of the fifth inning, Ethan went to find us food and more drinks. I stayed at our seats and texted Lauren to complain because I knew she'd understand.

"Here you go." Ethan handed me a hotdog and a Blue Moon. "Hope these are okay."

"How much was everything?"

"Don't worry about it."

I passive aggressively enjoyed my hotdog and waited for the game to end. I wanted to be anywhere else, but even with the discount, the seats weren't cheap. So, I sat in silence until they won. At least we had that going for us. After the game, we went to a dive bar down the street where I drank too much, so Ethan called us an Uber back into the city. My last memory of the night was falling asleep in the back seat.

~

Morning came and I was upset that I let a small argument get in the way of Ethan's last night in the city. He would be leaving a few hours later and I wished that I could press rewind and start the weekend over again.

"I wish you could stay." I rolled over and positioned my body closer to his.

"Me too." He stroked my hair.

"I'm scared for us, Ethan," I said. I was usually afraid of being vulnerable with him, but the words just slipped right out of my mouth before I could stop them.

"Why?" he asked.

"I don't know. This weekend just felt… different. I miss how things used to be."

He stayed silent for a minute.

"Change isn't always a bad thing. You seem happy here and I'm happy for you. I had a lot of fun." He kissed my forehead.

"I am, but you make me really happy too." I turned around and kissed him.

I proceeded to kiss him as I got on and took off his shirt. I wanted him to know how much he meant to me, and I knew how much he loved morning sex, so that felt like the best way to show him. Afterward, we went to brunch and then came back to the apartment so he could pack his things and call an Uber.

"Graham's doing his annual fourth of July party if you guys wanted to come," Ethan suggested.

"I'll see what days I get off. PTO doesn't start until 90 days in." I frowned.

"Stop that." He reached for my face and with his fingers, curved the corners of my mouth upward. "You're too cute to be angry."

I rolled my eyes and kissed him.

"Alright, my ride is here," he said.

I followed him downstairs to the street where his car was waiting. I really hated goodbyes and this one was proving worse than I'd expected. Ethan pulled me in, and we stayed like that for a minute or two before he kissed me one last time.

"See you soon, Hart."

I watched the car drive away and a tear fell down my cheek. Why did this have to be so hard? Our relationship had always been hard, and I was ready for it to be easy. Didn't we at least deserve that?

When I got back into the apartment, I was glad Lauren wasn't home. I cried in the shower and then turned on my comfort show, *Sex and the City*. I needed a lot of comfort at that moment, and nothing made me feel better than the mess that was Carrie Bradshaw's love life.

It was almost 8 p.m. and I hadn't heard from Ethan. I assumed that he had made it home safely but sent a text to be sure. He didn't fly too often, so maybe he just didn't realize what texting etiquette was like when it came to taking off and landing. I always text all my group chats, both parents and Ethan. Just so they know I didn't die or anything. After two more hours and three unanswered messages, he finally replied. I scanned the first few words of one of the longest texts I think I had ever received, and my heart dropped into my stomach.

Ethan Brady: I'm sorry to do this over text, but I couldn't find the words earlier. I don't think this is something I can do anymore. I feel so bad saying that, but you deserve someone who's ready to go all in with you, I'm just not there yet. I don't know if I'll ever be. I never pictured myself in a relationship or getting married but when you came along, I was confused. I still am. I want what's best for you and I'm not it. I have problems that you don't want to get involved in and as much as it kills me I know I have to let you go. You deserve so much more than me.

My hands were shaking as I read the message over and over. I paced my bedroom and debated how I wanted to handle this. Before I knew it, I was dialing Ethan's phone number and waiting for him to pick up my call.

"Are you fucking kidding me? Seriously Ethan?" I yelled.

"Sloane, I'm—"

"Don't even. Don't even say it. You were here all weekend. We fucked, I basically paid for everything on top of buying those Yankee tickets and you couldn't even work up the courage to break up with me in person? Do you know how pathetic that is?" I interrupted before he could even finish his sentence.

"I know," he sighed. "I wanted to. I just— I couldn't."

"Well, that's a great excuse. I hate you. I really hate you; you know that?" I started to sob.

"I'm sorry Sloane. I'm so sorry."

I hung up and threw my phone against the wall. I turned around and Lauren was standing in the doorway wide-eyed, like she'd just seen a ghost. She walked towards me and wrapped me in a hug which made me cry even more. I hated how powerless and fragile he made me feel.

"I'm sorry babe." She broke away from the hug to pick up my phone and make sure it wasn't broken. Unfortunately, it wasn't. "Do you want some space?"

"Can we drink wine and watch reality TV until I'm ready to talk about it?" I asked.

"Of course."

After a lot more tears and two glasses of wine, I told Lauren everything.

"Some people just aren't ready, no matter how much time you give them. Nothing will change until they decide they're ready," Lauren explained. "But here's the thing— you can't wait for them. You can't keep choosing someone who doesn't choose you."

"But I love him." I started crying again. "I've never loved anyone like this before."

"You're gonna hate to hear this, Sloane, but we're so young. Your person is out there and they're going to be your person for the rest of your life. You won't have to worry about this one foot in, one foot out situation with them. They're going to choose you and they're going to stay. Forever."

"I just wanted it to be Ethan."

"I know you did."

I crawled into bed, burrowed myself under the covers and tried to sleep. Even then, when I closed my eyes, all I saw was him. Isn't it funny how that happens? One day you don't know someone exists and the next you can't imagine a life without them.

Chapter 14

ETHAN · JUNE 2017

Sloane hung up on me. I didn't blame her, I guess. Why did I have to be the world's biggest dick and do that over text? Why couldn't I, for once in my life, just be vulnerable and honest? I owed that much to her; I knew that. I turned my phone off for the night and got in the shower.

Graham said there was a party at a brother's house in Wrightsville he wanted to go to, so I decided to join to take my mind off things. I'd love nothing more than to be drunk or stoned right now. After I showered, I threw on a Pike t-shirt, khaki shorts, and Nikes and found Graham cracking open a beer.

"You ready?" I asked.

"Grab a beer first." He nodded toward the fridge. I grabbed a Miller Lite and took a seat next to him on the couch. "So, what happened with Sloane?"

"Did she call you?" I asked.

"Dude, I could hear you on the phone. You weren't necessarily being quiet."

"I ended things with her." I knew Graham wouldn't give up until I told him. "I just felt like it was unfair to her."

"What was?" He took a sip of his beer.

"Leading her on when I can't date her. Not to mention the fact that we were long distance when we weren't even dating."

"Haven't we been here before? Why didn't you want to date her? I get the long distance thing, but I feel like it's more than that."

"I don't know. I really don't wanna talk or think about it anymore tonight."

Graham didn't press me any further. We finished our beers and once Jake got home from work, we headed to the party. Like most Wrightsville party houses, this one was a run-down shithole, and it was packed which was surprising for a Sunday summer night. Most girls were dressed in cut-off shorts and tops that resembled bikinis. I headed straight to the back deck where I knew I'd find brothers playing beer pong and that's where I stayed for the night.

I woke up the next morning on an unfamiliar couch. When my eyes finally adjusted, I realized I was still at the party house. A bong and remnants of weed sat on the coffee table in front of me, along with fast food wrappers and empty beer cans. I looked around and didn't see anyone else. I wondered where Graham was. I pulled my phone out to turn it on and get an Uber, expecting to see a text from Sloane. There wasn't one. What was I even expecting her to say? I shook the thought from my mind and put on my shoes as I waited for my driver to arrive.

The drive back to Ascent was quiet. As we crossed the

bridge, I remembered the time Sloane tried to convince me that the walk from Jerry's to our apartment was only a mile. In just a year, so many of our memories were written all over the town I'd lived my entire life in.

A wave of regret washed over me, and I began to question my decision-making skills. Had I made a mistake by breaking things off with Sloane? With a slight hangover, I tried to think rationally about everything.

Realistically speaking, even if I loved Sloane, we wouldn't work out. I was too messed up for her. I knew I couldn't give her what she wanted, and it wouldn't be fair to lead her on more than I already had. As much as it hurt, I know I did the right thing by ending things between us. The thought lingered in my head like a broken record until I finally arrived home. I knew it was the right choice, but it didn't make the pain any less real.

Chapter 15

SLOANE · JUNE 2017

No one talks about the morning after a breakup enough. Swollen eyes. Waking up— if you were lucky enough to sleep— wondering if it was just a nightmare. Realizing that it wasn't. The pain in your heart re-appearing. No 'good morning' text. No 'I'm sorry I fucked up' voicemail. Nothing. That was your new reality. A cold bed, an empty stomach and an ache in your chest that you fear will never go away.

I looked at myself in the front camera on my phone, because I didn't know if I'd be able to get out of bed. My eyes were the size of golf balls, I'm surprised I could even open them. There was no way I could keep my composure for an entire day in the office, and even if I could, my appearance would scare off all my new coworkers.

"Can you call in sick today?" Lauren stood at the end of my bed.

I hated lying, but I knew that was my only option. I handed Lauren my phone so she could send a message to Annie for me. I watch her type away, hit send and place the phone back on my bed.

"Do you want me to stay home?" she offered.

"We can't both lose our jobs." I let out a slight laugh.

"You know I'd stay if I could. Call me if you need anything— and don't start drinking until at least 2 p.m. okay?"

Once I heard the front door close, I grabbed my phone to call the one person that I know would make me feel better.

"Hello?" he answered.

"Hey, Graham," I replied.

"Everything okay? You never call this early."

"I'm okay. How are you?"

"Sloane, cut the shit. What's going on?" His tone was genuine.

"Ethan ended it, in a text," I managed between tears. "I just don't get it. Why wasn't I enough for him?"

"I think you're overthinking this. You and I both know it had nothing to do with being enough. Ethan's afraid of commitment. He refuses to let anyone get too close, and if I'm being honest, I'm surprised you made it this far."

"Thanks," I scoffed.

"You know I didn't mean it like that. I've known him almost my entire life and I've just never seen him let anyone in the way he has with you. Give him time; maybe he'll come back around."

"I don't want someone who comes back. I want someone who never leaves."

"Okay," he sighed. "I'm gonna be completely honest and tell you something he would kill me for sharing."

"What?"

"I still don't know all the details. When Ethan and I

were 13, both of his parents were arrested. They were drinking and driving, and they killed someone on a bike."

I was speechless, so he continued. "Ethan's dad had a few prior DUIs. He owned a hole-in-the-wall bar in the Carolina Beach area, so I think he'd drink a lot while he was there. According to rumors, there was a party at the bar the night of the accident, which is why Ethan's mom was also in the car. She was sentenced to a year, mostly for hiding information about the case, and his dad was sentenced to ten. When his mom was released, we all expected her to come back for him. That was the plan, according to Ethan. She never showed up and it broke him. He never said it, but we all knew. You could see it in everything he did. My mom tried to get in contact with her a few times, but she acts like that part of her life never existed. As far as my family knows, his mom moved somewhere in the Midwest, got re-married and has another kid. His dad gets out next year, but I don't think Ethan's in contact with him."

"Holy shit." I didn't know what to say.

"Yeah, so, that's pretty much everything. He's a good guy; he just has a lot of baggage— which is why I wanted to tell you this. It's not that he can't be with you, it's that he can't be with anyone. He doesn't know how to. Does any of this help? Or did I make things worse?"

"Yeah, it helps a lot. I just feel bad that I didn't see it. How could I not see it?"

"You can't blame yourself. Remember, you know none of this. It's not something you need to address, but I was hoping it would make you see his side of things. He has a lot of work on himself to do, but I like you for him."

"Thanks, Graham, you're a great guy." I wiped a tear

from my cheek as I hung up the phone.

My thoughts were racing at a million miles per minute as I tried to make sense of the situation. His parents' abandonment had left him with emotional scars that made him hesitant to get close to anyone, including me. How could I expect him not to be afraid of commitment after what he went through?

While it hurt to hear, I found some solace in knowing that it wasn't me. It wasn't my inadequacy that prevented him from loving me. It was his own self-doubt and fear of being abandoned. He didn't love himself enough to believe that he was worthy of someone who would stick around.

Despite the pain and heartbreak he'd caused me, I couldn't help but feel bad for him. I knew how difficult it was to overcome past traumas, and I hoped that one day he would find the courage to confront his fears and allow himself to love and be loved.

~

After a lot of wine and Taylor Swift's latest album on repeat, I felt okay enough to go back to work. I sat in my cubicle, pulled out my laptop and wondered if I'd be able to focus on anything else besides Ethan. Then, I noticed a bouquet of flowers next to my computer monitor. I grabbed the note that was tucked inside and read it.

Sloane, a card and flowers can't make this better, but I'm giving them to you anyway. XO, Annie.

How did Annie know about my breakup? I sorted through my tote bag until I found my phone and immediately pulled up the message Lauren had sent to her yesterday on my behalf.

Me: Hi Annie, this is Sloane's roommate. To be completely honest, she got broken up with last night and isn't doing too well. She really needs to take the day. Hope you understand!

"Got a sec?" Annie appeared.

"I'm so sorry about this." I held up my phone that was open to our text conversation. "I had no idea."

"Don't be sorry, I appreciate the honesty. You have a great roommate." She leaned on the edge of my desk. "Your 20s are hard, and breakups are no joke. Take the time you need to grieve it, but don't be afraid of putting this experience into your work. Use it as fuel when you write. Nothing says revenge like virality."

Annie was right. I plugged my laptop into the monitor and sent Mila a meeting invitation for that afternoon.

"Break up brainstorm?" Her head popped up over the half wall that separated us. "What happened?"

"Long story short, he's not ready. I'm not sure that he'll ever be."

"I'm sorry, that sucks. Well, I've never actually been dumped, but I can imagine that it sucks."

"You've never been dumped?"

"Nope, I end it with them before they have the chance to do the same. Saves me a whole lot of heartbreak."

"Save it for the brainstorm sesh." I laughed and shooed her away.

"See ya in a few!" She disappeared back into her cube.

I thought back to just a few months earlier when I was worried that I'd never land a job in the city. Not only did

I find a job, but I was getting paid to write about my breakup. It scared me a little, how everything was falling into place.

"Let's start with some topics." Mila stood in front of a whiteboard.

"If we want the readers to follow the journey of the breakup, I'm thinking we start with something small and work our way into the deeper stuff," I explain. "Maybe like, we've made a post-break-up playlist, so you don't have to?"

"Genius," she said. "What's next?"

"Our best break-up advice, before you get into an almost relationship read this, an open letter to the guy who didn't want to date me."

We sat in that conference room until well past 5 p.m. spewing off advice, stories from past relationships, and things we've read or watched in movies that stuck with us.

I spent the entire subway ride home writing articles piece by piece in the notes app on my phone. I swear, if anyone ever had access to these, I'd personally dig my own grave and bury myself in there. Midnight thoughts, drunk rants, things I'll never tell anyone. Good thing they're password protected now with Apple's latest update.

~

In the weeks that followed, I continued to throw myself into work. I stayed late at the office, wrote article after article, and guest-starred on a few podcasts in our network. I finally started to feel at peace with the fact that Ethan and I were never meant to last. It hurt, but it was true.

"Sloane! Your article hit a million reads!" Annie shouted from her office.

Everyone in their surrounding cubicles cheered and congratulated me. I couldn't help but cry. Mila handed me a few tissues and hugged me.

"I'm so proud of you," she said.

"You helped make this happen," I replied.

I shared the article "An Open Letter to the Guy Who Didn't Want to Date Me" on my personal social media channels before Annie told me to go home and use the afternoon as a personal day. I didn't argue. Instead, I treated myself to a manicure and a glass of wine until Lauren got done nannying and could meet me for a drink.

"I'll take a bottle of Veuve," Lauren ordered.

"Laur, that's expensive. Let me split it," I insisted.

"I'm so proud of you. Just let me get this, okay?"

After finishing the bottle of champagne, we ended up at a piano bar on the Upper East Side right around the corner from our apartment.

"We need more friends in the city." Lauren sighed as we settled into a two-top near the window. "This would be the perfect night to go out, like really out! Not just to a bar on our street."

"Who else do we know here?" I said, scrolling through all my unopened messages to see if I'd missed any.

"No clue." Lauren rolled her eyes and took a swig of her vodka soda.

My phone vibrated on the table and while I'd usually try to be respectful and not check it, I picked it up immediately in hopes that it was someone that I'd been waiting on. Instead, it was the last person I'd expect to hear from— Reese.

Reese Thompson: Hey there. Heard you moved to the city. Congrats on everything. Also saw your viral article. Are you free for drinks or dinner this week?

"Oh my gosh."

"What?" Lauren asked. "Ethan?"

"No… Reese."

"Stop! You're gonna answer right? Wait, I bet he has roommates. Tell them to come out tonight!" Lauren begged.

"Fine." I laughed. Clearly, he was still into me. What did I have to lose?

An hour and a half and two more vodka sodas later, Lauren and I were waiting in line at Gem Saloon in Murray Hill. Since we only moved to the city a month ago and lived all the way in Upper East Side, we didn't have much time to explore places outside of our neighborhood yet. According to Reese, Gem was one of the better weeknight spots.

"I'm nervous," I said to Lauren as the line slowly inched forward.

"Don't be! Reese is great. Plus, he was like obsessed with you so that's a plus," she said.

"Oh, was I?" a voice replied from behind us. I spun around and there he was— Reese Thompson in the flesh.

"Kidding! Hey, Reese!" Lauren hugged him and proceeded to introduce herself to his friends.

"Hey you." He side-hugged me.

"Sorry about all of that." I blushed.

"Don't worry about it, it was flattering. Now follow me, I know the bouncers." Reese grabbed my hand and led us all to the front of the line. He handed him a wad of cash and we were given the head nod approval to make our way inside.

Gem Saloon was just like any other hole-in-the-wall bar except it was decently sized and had a ton of windows. Which seemed rare for New York. We followed him to the main bar, where he ordered a round of drinks and shots. The entire time he held onto my hand, and I realized that I didn't want him to let go.

That night I realized that losing someone doesn't necessarily mean losing. Every time someone walks out of your life, someone new eventually walks into it. Losing someone means you'll eventually gain someone even better.

Part 2

NOW · 7 MONTHS LATER

Chapter 16

SLOANE · JANUARY 2018

The subway is nearly empty on my way home from work.
Our office has been open since the day after New Year's,
but everyone knows that people with kids don't go back
to work until the second week of January when school
starts back up again. I get off at my new stop, 23rd and 3rd
and walked up two blocks. Our new building is a complex
on 25th, complete with a community laundromat, gym and
a doorman.

Annie sends me a text asking me to cover an event
tonight because she wouldn't make it back from New
Jersey in time. It's a launch party for a new skincare
company, so I knew there'd be a lot of free samples. I
agree and start typing the details into my calendar when
the crosswalk brings me to a complete halt. I shove my
phone into my bag and watch for the walk signal— that's
when I see him.

Why is he here?

Why is he wearing a suit and carrying a backpack?

Is he here for work?

What does he even do for work?

Does he live here now?

No way, that's impossible.

He'd never move to New York. He said it himself.

We held eye contact for a brief second and then the signal changes. I half expect him not to cross the street and wait for me so he can explain what the hell he's doing in the middle of Manhattan, the last place I ever expected to see him. Instead, we brush past each other just like every other stranger that has somewhere to be.

~

"I can't believe he'd move to New York and not tell you! I could kill him. I mean, who does that?" Lauren hisses.

"Hold on, I need a drink for this conversation," I reply.

The kitchen in our new apartment is much nicer than the last. It has a standard sized refrigerator and a decently sized island, which is perfect for entertaining. I walk over to the kitchen, grab a wine glass and fill it to the rim.

"Okay, continue," I say, taking a sip.

"Start from the beginning," she says. "Where did you see him?"

"It felt like that scene in Gossip Girl when Blair was in that taxi in Paris and saw Chuck on the corner," I explain.

"Did you talk?"

"That was the worst part. It was like we were strangers."

"Okay, so then it's not technically confirmed that he even lives here. He could be here on a work trip or something. Let's check his LinkedIn." Lauren runs to her room to get her laptop.

One of my favorite things about her is how quickly she

can dig up information on anyone. If you give her five minutes she'll know their address, phone number, mother's maiden name and three most recent exes. I always joke that she should've been a criminal justice major so she could work for the F.B.I. or a private investigator.

"Ethan Brady," she reads simultaneously while typing. "Digital Production Assistant at NBC Sports New York. How does someone like him get a job like that? No offense."

"Graham," we both say in unison.

"That's the only answer. His dad knows everyone."

"This makes me hate men more than I already do. They always get everything handed to them."

"Is he kidding?" I start. "He could go anywhere in the entire country, even the world probably, and he chooses here? What kind of person does that? Also, what are the odds of us running into each other like that? Am I being pranked?"

"Calm down," she laughs. "Realistically, you're probably never going to see him again. That run-in was the universe's way of letting you know that he lives here."

"I would've preferred to see a tweet or Instagram story over running into him on our street. But yeah, you're probably right." I sigh. "Will you go with me to a work event tonight? It's a launch party for a new skincare brand and I'm covering it. I bet their swag bags will be good."

"You had me at free booze, but a swag bag? Now I'm a thousand percent in."

"Good, get ready. We'll grab apps on our way."

My bedroom is half the size of the one in our Upper Eastside sublet, but the kitchen and living room is where we spend most of our time. Our new building is in Murray Hill, within walking distance of all our favorite coffee shops, restaurants, and bars. We're finally living the post-grad life we dreamt of.

In the tiny room, I'm able to fit a vanity, which is a necessity since we share a bathroom with a pedestal sink. I take a seat on the stool and look at myself in the mirror. I think back to when I would get ready in college; my face was a little fuller and my eyes a little brighter. After the move and breakup, I lost a little bit of weight. You could tell the most in my face— my cheeks and jaw are more defined now, which I think makes me look more mature. I turn on a playlist as I reapply mascara, blush, and a light coat of lipstick. Seconds into the first song my phone starts vibrating.

Incoming call: Reese Thompson

"Hey," I answer.

"Hey! Busy tonight? I got off earlier than I expected to and was thinking we could try that new cocktail lounge around the corner from my place." I could hear the hustle and bustle of the city in the background, which told me he likely just stepped out of the building.

Reese is like no one I've ever met. He's attentive, always makes plans for us and he's great at communicating. Almost too good at it. Reese is the opposite of Ethan. Things with Reese are simple and fun, which is why I like him. Some days I think that I could maybe love him down the road but right now, I'm still not over Ethan. Seeing him today proved that.

"Annie has me covering a collab launch event tonight

that Lauren's tagging along to. I wish I could though," I reply.

"Shit, I'm sorry, baby."

Baby. God, I hate pet names.

"It's okay. Maybe this weekend?"

"It's a date. Good luck tonight; call me when you get home if you want. I'm just gonna catch up on some work after I eat."

"Sounds good. I'll call you later." I put the phone down and walk back out to the common area. I need to get out of this apartment and into an establishment with alcohol and music. Stat.

~

The party is stunning. Upon arrival, a server hands us each a glass of champagne and a branded card with the night's agenda on it. It's being held at a bar in the Moxy Hotel and the room is full of lifestyle, beauty, and fashion editors. I already knew it'd be all I'll see on Instagram for the next forty-eight hours.

"I would kill for your job," Lauren says as she reaches for another glass of champagne from the display wall. "Tonight, I'll pretend I'm a big-shot fashion editor. Tomorrow, it'll be back to running around Tribeca with two little gremlins."

Lauren accepted a job as an elementary school teacher in the Bronx when we first moved to the city. She knew it would be hard; she'd make just above minimum wage and the commute wasn't the best. The reason she majored in education wasn't for the money, it was to have an impact on underprivileged children. To pass the time until the school year started, she found a full-time nanny job with the Bauer family. She spent the entire summer with their two five-year-old twin boys and come Labor Day she resigned from the teaching job to continue nannying. They feel like her home away from home— on most days anyway.

"Oh, stop it, they're not gremlins."

"I know, they're so cute. William won his soccer game yesterday and was so proud of himself. I'm sure it will be all he talks about tomorrow."

"That sentence just made me feel like we're 40-year-old moms having our monthly GNO." I laugh.

"Touché. Let's get martinis and mingle. Who should we talk to first?"

We approach the bar and order two extra dirty martinis, mine with olives and Lauren's without, then I scan to see if I notice any familiar faces.

"I see the head of marketing over in the corner. I'm going to grab a few pictures and a statement from her for our Instagram. Make us some new friends!"

I leave Lauren and nervously walk toward the group of people I only know by association. After an hour of small talk, I find Lauren sitting at the bar wrapped up in conversation.

"Hey, are you ready to go home?" I say, tapping her shoulder.

"I think I'm gonna stay, I have a late start tomorrow morning." She turns to me and throws a slight head nod to the guy sitting next to her. "Text me when you get to the apartment!"

I hand her the rest of my drink, knowing it'll go to waste otherwise, and pull out my phone to call an Uber. There's no way I'm taking the subway this late alone. I'm not that much of a New Yorker yet. The car pulls up to our building and I notice our doorman perched right behind the double doors. Doormen are one of my favorite things about the city— they make me feel safe like I'm coming home from a date to my dad waiting up for me on the couch.

"Thanks, Phillip!" I greet him as I step through the open door and into the lobby.

"Pleasure's all mine, Sloane. Want me to get your mail while you're here? Unit 13A, correct?"

"Sure, that'd be great." I pull out my phone to text Lauren that I've made it home when I hear the buzzer that signifies someone is entering the building. Out of instinct, I look up, and there he is. Again. My heart is now in my stomach.

"Hi, Sloane."

It's him. It's really him.

Something about hearing him speak makes it real. I'd know that voice anywhere. He isn't just a figure in my imagination. Ethan Brady is standing right in front of me, in my apartment building.

"Hi," I manage, surprised that I can even form words.

"I guess now would be a good time to tell you I moved to New York, and by the looks of it, I moved into your building," he says, barely able to look at me.

"You live here?" I stutter.

Phillip returns and realizes that he interrupted something. He sets my mail at the front desk and walks back to his office.

"I thought you were in the Upper East Side? But yes, Sloane, I live here." I hate how he says my name like he's using it against me.

"The couple we were leasing from came back to the

city, after their time abroad. We moved here a few weeks ago, around Christmas," I state.

"I don't know what to say," he started. "I heard about this place from some buddies at work. They've been wanting to get out of Brooklyn but needed a third roommate to afford this building, so when I joined the team, they recruited me. I had no idea you lived here though."

I'm searching for every bit of willpower I have to stop myself from telling him that I've missed him. To tell him that it doesn't matter if he didn't tell me, at least he's here now. But I can't say either of those things.

"You didn't think to reach out when you accepted a job offer in New York?" is what I say instead.

"I was going to. I wanted to. I didn't know what to say."

"Hey Sloane, just wanted to let you know I'm moving to New York?" I suggested.

"I'm sorry, I should've said something. I didn't want to open this up again and make it a whole thing." He avoids eye contact.

"Well, it's definitely a 'whole thing' now."

It's funny how people don't change. I mean, not really. He still has those same piercing brown eyes that somehow both comfort me and break my heart at the same time. When I stare into them, I see the cotton candy skies that drenched the windows at the mountain house. I see streetlights glistening through the windshield on our drives over the bridge. His eyes make me feel like I'm back in those places, in those exact moments. I miss those moments. I miss him. Even now, when I've had enough time to get over him. How did we end up here?

I turn my back to him and hightail it to the elevator. I feel a lump of emotion work its way to the back of my throat and tears form in my eyes. When I finally reach the fourth floor, I can't hold it in any longer and I start sobbing.

Until Lauren gets home, I sit on the couch in the dark replaying the entire run-in in my head.

"Oh, Sloane," I hear Lauren say as she walks into the living room. "I'm so sorry."

"Why can't I just forget him already? Why does he have to keep popping up in places like our fucking apartment building? I can't be neighbors with him again Lauren, I can't do it. I can barely stand to see his face without wanting to cry. How is this supposed to work?" I cry.

"Listen to me." Lauren grabs my face so I'm looking at her. "You're never going to forget him. A part of you will always love him. One day you'll find yourself searching for someone who reminds you of the best parts of him. You might never fully get over him, but you're going to be okay."

"Thanks, Laur." I wipe a tear from my cheek. "Do you think Graham knew? I would've thought he'd warn me."

"At the end of the day, Graham only cares about himself. I'm sure he's too wrapped up in his new girlfriend to think about you and Ethan," she says coldly and stands up.

"You're right." I reach my arm out so she can help me up. "I hate both of them so much."

"As you should." Lauren laughs a little.

Chapter 17

ETHAN · JANUARY 2018

Fuck.

Fuck, fuck, fuck.

How are we living in the same building? Isn't this supposed to be the most populated city in America? If she didn't already, she hates me now.

I set my takeout on the counter and don't even feel like eating anymore, which is very unlike me since I never pass up a meal. My roommates, Noah and Lucas, seem to still be out, so I strip down to just my boxers in the hall and head into the bathroom. The scalding hot water hits my back as I stand in the stall shower and think about everything Sloane and I have been through the past two years.

After I finish recounting the weirdest two years of my life, I heat up the Chipotle bowl and sit on the couch to eat it. Scrolling Netflix, I realize there's nothing new I haven't watched so I decide to FaceTime Graham.

"Look who it is!" he answers.

"Is it Ethan? How's the city?" Emily appears from

behind Graham with a huge smile.

"Hey Em," I greet her. "It's fucking cold."

"It's January. Besides that, everything good?" Graham asks. "How's work? Roommates?"

"Work's great, roommates are cool." I pause. "There is one thing though…"

"What?"

"So, uh, Sloane lives in my building."

"What?" His mouth hangs open. "You're fucking with me. Right?"

"Dude, I wish."

"How'd you find out?" he asks.

So, I tell him the entire story from start to finish—from spotting her on the street, to the awkward lobby encounter.

"Are you guys gonna talk about it?"

"Probably not." I shrug.

"I don't understand you."

"Neither do I."

We hang up and I stare at the black TV screen. I wonder where Noah and Lucas are. I shoot a text in our group chat, hoping if they're out they'll stay there for a while. I could use a drink.

~

"There he is!" Noah waves me down. "Grab a beer from the bucket, you've got winner."

Darts are such a New York City thing. I don't think even one bar in Wilmington has them, at least none I've been to.

"So, how's your first official week in the city? Work kicking your ass yet?" Lucas asks.

"It's going. Luckily not yet," I reply.

"Screw you, Lucas," Noah says, pulling the darts from the board. "Brady, you're up."

"Anyone ever tell you that you're a sore loser?" Lucas mocks Noah.

"Every damn day."

Even though I've only been living here for exactly eight days, I can already tell I'm going to like it. I never pictured myself as a city guy, but I also never thought I'd land a job like this. I was grateful to the Clarks for providing me with a family and a life I didn't think I was worthy of. I've always been afraid of it but I think I'm realizing that change is a good thing. A really good thing.

Chapter 18

SLOANE · FEBRUARY 2018

Reese smiles at me from across the table and then takes a sip from his wine glass. I move around the lettuce on my plate while he rambles on about new clients. I'm surprised that he hasn't realized how checked out I've been all night.

It's Valentine's Day. I've never celebrated this day with anyone, except Lauren of course. He made this reservation three months in advance, sent a dozen roses to my office and was waiting outside of my building when I got off work. I can't help but feel like I'm betraying him.

Since I found out that Ethan's my neighbor, I've been questioning my relationship with Reese. He has no idea about any of this, because I wanted to give myself time to process it all. It's been a little over a month and I still can't bring myself to tell him. Things with Reese are easy in a way they never were with Ethan. Our relationship is secure and predictable. So why doesn't it feel like enough?

"After this deal closes, I want to take you out of the

city for a weekend," he says. "We haven't been on a trip together yet."

"That would be nice," I say as I put my napkin over the hardly eaten salad.

"Where should we go? Somewhere warm?"

"Yes! Somewhere with a beach. I miss the beach."

"Did you not like your food? Order something else," he offers.

"I'm not that hungry, I had a late lunch." I hate lying to him.

Reese has become familiar. I've gotten used to falling asleep next to him at night. I like the way he smells fresh out of the shower and how it feels when he wraps his arms around me. We spend weeknights ordering in and weekends exploring the city. He gives me the kind of relationship I convinced myself for so long that I wasn't deserving of.

"I was thinking we could go back to Wilmington. My parents usually spend the spring at our rental in Kure Beach and I'd really like you to meet them."

The wine, mixed with my overwhelming sense of shock, causes me to swallow wrong and I start coughing. I can't go back to Wilmington with him. I haven't even been back there myself since graduation. That entire town has Ethan written all over it. It's where I fell in love for the first and last time.

"Sorry, wrong pipe I guess." I lift the napkin to my mouth. "That could be fun."

"Think on it. I'll go wherever you want." He smiles and motions for the server to bring the check. "Should we stay at your place tonight? I feel bad that you've been coming to mine a lot. Work should slow down soon."

"We can do yours again, my sheets are still in the dryer." Here I go again, lying.

I can't bear the thought of sleeping under the same roof as Ethan with Reese in my bed. Something about it just feels... Wrong.

On the few and far between nights that I've slept at my own apartment, I've laid in bed wondering if he's staring at the same ceiling fan that I am. It's like looking at the stars knowing the person you're missing shares the same sky as you, wondering if when they look up, you come to their mind too.

I just can't seem to comprehend how this has happened. Over eight million people live in this fucking city, and I wind up living in the same building as the only guy that's ever broken my heart. How is that possible? At first, I thought maybe it was a sign. Maybe we were meant to be. I quickly realized that sometimes not every coincidence or run-in at the grocery store must mean something. Sometimes, you really do end up in the same place at the same time as someone you don't want to see by chance. And there are two ways to handle it.

Option one: convince yourself this was on purpose and try to figure out the said purpose.

Option two: realize it was a coincidence and continue with your life.

I sleep at Reese's for the rest of the week to avoid the thought of Ethan. When I'm in this bubble, alone with Reese, things are great. When I'm alone, that's when I start to spiral.

~

"Brought you coffee, baby." I open my eyes to Reese sitting on the edge of his bed, stroking my arm to wake

131

me. "I've gotta get to that cycling thing with the guys but let me know what you get into tonight. We can all meet up."

He leaves a key on the counter for me, and I roll over in his bed. Sometimes, it feels wrong to be here. To know that he likes me more than I like him. I reach over to the nightstand for my phone as it starts vibrating in my hand.

"Hello?" I answer without looking at who it is.

"I haven't seen you all week! It feels like I live alone now. Brunch?" Lauren asks. "A few of the girls from my nanny group are meeting in midtown and added us to the res. Can you be home and ready in an hour?"

"Yeah, I'll see you in a few." I hang up and quickly get out of bed.

I brush my teeth with the pink electric toothbrush Reese bought for me that matches his blue one. I'm wearing one of his t-shirts paired with the leftover mascara that I was too lazy to take off last night. I sigh as I stare at the confused girl that looks back at me in the mirror. Why can't I just be content with him? Why can't I like him the way he likes me?

Is love being content with someone? I know that love isn't settling just because the person you're with loves you the way you've always loved other people. I fully believe that for a relationship to last a lifetime, you both need to be infatuated with each other. And as much as I try, I worry that I'll never feel that way about Reese.

Lauren and I walk into brunch less than five minutes late, which is record timing for her. Usually, whatever time Lauren says we're leaving is delayed by at least twenty minutes. That time consists of at least four outfit changes, misplacing her phone or I.D., and touching up her makeup. I don't consider myself a patient person but with Lauren, I have to be. I don't mind waiting on her, well, most days anyway.

"Here they are!" one of the girls narrates our entrance. "Brunch officially starts now."

In New York City, bottomless brunch gets timed. Typically, you have about one and a half to two hours per table so you can't sit there all day with a $40 total tab. Servers have to make money somehow, and bottomless brunch and tips from drunk patrons is how they do it. Not even a few minutes into brunch, I get a text from Annie, which is out of character for a Saturday afternoon.

Annie Walker: Hate to ask but any chance you can go to Boston later this week for me? Kids are sick. LMK.

A wave of relief washes over me. I can't wait for a few days away from the city. I couldn't think of a better way to clear my head. I've never been to Boston. I couldn't wait to go and explore the city on my own.

"Who's that? Reese?" Lauren gushes over him.

"No, it's work. I have to go to Boston tomorrow night to fill in for Annie at a conference."

"Boo," she pouts.

"Let's hit Lower East Side next! I bet we can find some good live music there," one of the girls interrupts us.

We head to the subway after hitting our time limit at brunch. I've already had a lot to drink but figure one or two more couldn't hurt. Besides Lauren and Mila, I don't have any friends in the city. When we first moved here, I was putting all my effort into work and long distance with Ethan. Once that ended, I was focused on work and getting over Ethan. I wish I'd realized the importance of making friends in such a big city.

I'm two more drinks in when I feel my phone vibrating in my back pocket.

Incoming Call: Reese Thompson

I let it go to voicemail and see that I have three unread text messages from him.

Reese Thompson: We're pregaming Gem.
Reese Thompson: Got a table in the front.
Reese Thompson: Miss you baby.

Those texts make me want to take a shot. Or five. Something about the amount of alcohol I'm drinking makes me want to think of Ethan and forget about Reese. It's fucked up, I know. I can't help it. Before putting my phone away again, I check social media to see if Ethan's posted any stories today. Nothing.

Maybe I should just reach out to him? I'm fighting an internal battle that I know I can't vocalize to Lauren because she'll tell me not to text him. Which is exactly what I should do. Do not text Ethan. Yet, I hit send anyway.

~

Less than an hour later, I'm in Ethan's apartment, which is just a floor above my own. It feels like Ascent all over again. I wonder if he ever thinks about that.

I take a seat on the couch and the worn-out leather feels cold on my legs. Even though it's the height of winter, my favorite going-out outfit combination is a skirt, tights, bodysuit, and tall boots. Thank God for New York City coat checks. I glance around the apartment, taking in every detail. Mismatched furniture that I'm sure he got off a curb, two TVs for an optimal football Sunday experience, and blank walls with absolutely no decor.

"Want a drink?" Ethan shouts from the kitchen.

"Sure," I say, even though I know I'm past my limit. Way past my limit.

"All I've got is whiskey," he replies.

This isn't going to end well.

He takes a seat on the other side of the couch, and it feels like we're worlds apart. This living room might feel small, but it fits one of the biggest sections I've ever seen, so I'll give it that. I take a sip of Jameson as my eyes wander around the room a bit more, waiting for him to break the ice. Just a few months ago we were able to just exist together without saying anything and now we're trying to find any words to fill the silence.

"I'm sorry again, for all of this," he finally apologizes.

"It's okay, you didn't know," I reassure him, as I always do.

"I mean, I knew you lived in the city. The least I could've done was text you."

"You're not wrong."

"So, why'd you text me?" he asks. "Was that all you wanted? An apology?

"Can't answer that."

"Why not?"

"This isn't my first drink tonight, Ethan." I wave around my drink and some spills out.

"Alright, alright. Give me that." He scoots closer and reaches for the glass.

"No way!" I tilt my body away from his, holding the glass of whiskey high in the air and as far away from his reach as I can get. He grabs it and places it on the coffee table while positioning his body on top of mine.

"Sloane," he starts. "I've hated myself for so long for what I did to you. I never wanted to hurt you."

"I know. The sad part is, as much as I tried, I couldn't hate you. I don't think I'll ever be able to hate you."

In an instant, his hand grips my thigh, and his face is within inches of mine. My cheeks go flush, and my heart rate heightens. This is what Ethan does to me every time.

"Hi," I say nervously.

"Hi," he says into my hair. "Is this okay? Can I kiss you?"

I remember when I was his and he didn't have to ask if what he was doing was okay— he could just do it because .he knew that I wanted him to. I hate these questions.

I know I shouldn't let him kiss me, but I do it anyway. "Yes." What does that say about me?

Maybe I'm hoping that if we kiss and there aren't sparks, or the chemistry isn't there anymore, and that will be reason enough for me to let go. I know I've tried to move on and I have a little, thanks to Reese, but somehow he still has this hold on me that I can't explain.

I pull him in, and our lips meet for the first time in what feels like years, but they find their way to each other like it was just yesterday. Kissing Ethan makes me feel undone. I'm high. I'm floating. And then, I'm not. Suddenly, reality sets back in. Ethan broke my heart. Reese put it back together. What the fuck am I doing?

"I have a boyfriend," I announce and pull away.

"A boyfriend?" He sits up, confused.

"What did you expect from me? You broke up with me in a text and I never heard from you again. Did you think I'd wait for you to just call or something?" I back up so that I'm sitting up straight.

"No, no. I know that. I guess I was selfishly hoping that you wouldn't move on."

"Well, I did. After I stopped comparing everyone to you."

"So then why are you here?"

I don't know how to answer that. I stand up and collect myself, scanning the room for where I left my purse. I grab it off the recliner and walk towards the front door, waiting for him to tell me to stop. He doesn't. I grab the handle and still nothing. As it closes behind me, a tear falls down my cheek. How am I back here again? Almost two years of moving on and I was right back to feeling the same way I did the morning he left for the airport. Extremely confused and sad. I head down the single-flight stairs that led to my apartment and pull out my phone to call Reese.

"Hey!" he shouts over loud music.

"Can you come over?"

"I thought you'd never ask. Unlock the door, I'm on my way." He hangs up.

I change into my favorite matching sweat set and freshen up so he can't tell that I had been crying. As I wipe the mascara from under my eyes, I stare at my reflection in the same way I did this morning and wonder who I've become. I'm in love with someone who can't love me back and has told me that more times than I can count. Reese is sure about me. His feelings for me have never wavered and that's all I've ever wanted. So why can't it be enough?

"Sloane?" Reese calls out.

"In here!"

He sits on my bed and reaches his arms out, motioning for me to join him. I stand in between his legs and place both of my hands on his shoulders. His hands rest on my waist and he looks up at me, waiting for me to kiss him. Kissing Reese is different than kissing Ethan. It's more gentle and less passionate.

I kiss him harder and wait for his mouth to follow. He catches up and slides one hand under the front of my shirt. Then I feel his other move up my back and unclasp my bra before maneuvering it and my sweatshirt off me. Finally, he takes charge. I move from his lap and lay on his bed, wiggling my pants and underwear past my ankles as he leans over to grab a condom from my bedside table. I never used condoms with Ethan, but Reese almost always insists.

Sex with Reese is fine. Just that— fine. I think about Ethan a lot while I'm having sex with Reese. It's fucked up, I know, but I can't help it. I often wonder if I'll ever feel the things that I felt with Ethan ever again. Is that the kind of love you only get once in your life? I re-insert myself into the present moment right as Reese is about to finish and I almost wish I hadn't.

"I love you baby," he whispers between breaths.

This is now the second time he's told me without waiting for me to reciprocate it. I grasp his body tighter and lightly dig my teeth into his shoulder to avoid having to respond right away. I need to delay a response for as long as I possibly can. I like Reese, sometimes I think I could even love him one day. Not in the way I love Ethan. I hate that I compare them so often, but I still don't know how not to compare everyone to Ethan.

He pulls back and kisses me before plopping his body next to mine. We lay there for a few minutes before I get up to go to the bathroom.

"Wait, not yet." He grabs my arm and tries to pull me back towards him.

"I have to pee."

I apologetically kiss his forearm and search for a shirt to wear before heading to the bathroom. I run the faucet water so Reese can't hear that I'm not using the bathroom as I stare at myself in the mirror. Partially ashamed, and mostly confused.

Why am I doing this?

"You good?" He knocks on the door. I flush the toilet and turn the doorknob to let him in.

"Had to wash my face," I explain.

"Come to bed."

Reese grabs both of my hands and pulls me so that my body is flush with his. His hands then find their way to my hips and then my butt. He hoists me up and carries me the entire twenty steps to my room. I think I could love him. We get into bed together and even though his body is inches from mine, I feel hundreds of miles away.

"Is something wrong?"

"No, why would it be?" I lie.

"I didn't want to bring this up, but I've told you I love you twice now and you haven't said it back. I was giving you some time to do it on your own, but I feel like we should talk about it."

I turn around so that I'm facing him. Even though the

room is dark, the streetlights peer through the blinds, allowing us to somewhat see each other's faces. I don't know how to answer his question, so I rely on yet another lie.

"Both times have been during sex. I want to say it when I feel it in a different moment."

"Shit, I'm sorry baby. I love you all the time, not just during sex." He grabs my face and kisses me.

~

"Where should we go for breakfast?" Reese wakes me up by rubbing his fingers over my cheek.

"I'm not that hungry." It's true. Since Ethan's been back, I haven't had much of an appetite. My anxiety doesn't let me.

"What if I said I was able to get us reservations at La Mercerie in an hour?" he says.

"Seriously?" I sit up almost immediately.

"Go get ready." He laughs.

We've been trying to get reservations there for weeks now. In college, Reese studied abroad and said that La Mercerie was the closest thing on the east coast to French pastries. So of course, I need to make sure he isn't overexaggerating.

We walk out of the elevator hand in hand and as I look up, there's Ethan. This can't be happening. How is this happening? We silently pass each other in the lobby. They were fraternity brothers for three years so they're both very aware of one another's existence. I stay quiet until Reese has the nerve to bring it up. I never did find the right time to tell him. An Uber pulls up and we awkwardly get inside. He drops my hand and immediately I know this brunch is about to be torturous.

"Really, Sloane? You're kidding me, right?" He raises his voice. I've never heard Reese angry before.

"I can expl—"

"I'm not doing this with you. This is fucking pathetic. Why is he here?" he asks again.

"Stop." I grab his hand again and motioned toward the driver who seems to be getting uncomfortable.

"What? You don't want to tell me what your ex is doing in the building that you live in?" He's yelling now.

"Reese, seriously stop."

"Sloane— why the fuck is he here? In New York?"

He pulls his hand out from underneath mine and turns away to look out the window. I can tell he's bracing himself for the answer he doesn't want.

"He lives here," I say quietly.

"In your building? This must be a joke. You're joking, right?" he's facing me again and this time he's visibly angry.

"I didn't know until recently. I ran into him a few blocks away and then again later that day in the lobby." I hide the fact that I've known for well over a month.

"Is he stalking you? How did he end up in your building?"

"It was a coincidence, I guess,"

"Bullshit. Nothing with that guy is ever coincidental. He's calculated and manipulative." He isn't wrong. "Have the two of you talked?"

There's absolutely no way I'm telling him the truth.

"Just the day I ran into him," I lie.

We're both quiet for the next few minutes and I wonder if this brunch will even happen anymore. I stare out the window as the city passes us by. Coffee shops and

141

restaurants we love, corners we've kissed on, crosswalks we've held hands at. Is this the end of us? If it is, I deserve it, I guess.

"I'm sorry," he sighs. "I feel like I'm overreacting. It just felt like a punch to the gut when you said you knew he lived here and didn't tell me. That's a big deal. You should've told me."

"I know." I put my hand on his thigh. "I'm sorry. I was trying to process it and figure out how to tell you. I should've just told you as soon as it happened."

"It's okay, I shouldn't have gotten so angry." He picks my hand up and intertwines his fingers with mine. "I love you, you know that, right?"

"I love you too."

I finally say it and I don't think it's a lie. The thought of losing him makes me realize that maybe I am falling in love with him. I squeeze his hand and then he kisses me.

Three words can change so much. Three words can make you completely forgive someone and forget why you were upset with them in the first place. Three words can make you feel like the most important person in the world.

Chapter 19

SLOANE · FEBRUARY 2018

I've always found peace in traveling alone. I love getting to the airport a little early even though I breeze through security with pre-check. My typical routine has been to find a bar and order a glass of Sauvignon Blanc and a side of fries while I people-watch and catch up on some work. That is of course until I met Ethan. Now, I can't step into an airport without wondering what it would be like to travel with him. Does he enjoy getting to the airport early or is he the kind of passenger who makes it to the gate right as they're boarding the last group? Does he read or sleep on the flight? Questions I've always hoped I'd know the answers to, but now I know that I never will.

I'm waiting to board my plane when I see the post on Instagram— Graham finally proposed to Emily. They met at his family's company party, where her dad is the head of marketing. The next morning, Graham sent me a text saying he'd met his wife. I can't believe some people just know that easily. I often wonder if that was the feeling that jolted through my body the moment that I met Ethan.

I'm so happy for them but I can't help but feel a little nostalgic and sad. I pictured Graham's wedding day going so much differently.

Ethan and I would be sharing a hotel room. I'd be putting on my dress while he was just getting in the shower. He'd blast Frank Sinatra and sing at an unreasonable volume because it always made me laugh. He'd try to dance with me, and I'd playfully push him off, careful that he didn't mess up my hair or makeup. I'd still let him kiss me though. I always let him kiss me.

"Now boarding group four," the gate agent comes over the loudspeaker.

Immediately I'm thrown back into reality, grab my bag and head for the line. I scan my boarding pass and find my way to seat 13A. I always choose a window seat and I used to wonder if that would have to change if I traveled with Ethan. Would I get comfortable in the middle seat? Or would we be that couple that sits across the aisle from each other? Now I'll never know. How is it that he's still such a prominent part of memories that I'm not even making with him?

Halfway through the flight, I get bored enough to start clearing out my camera roll, so I click to the top of the album. It shoots me up to my first ever iCloud photos, which happen to be junior year move-in day. I usually try to avoid looking back at photos of Ethan and I, but sometimes late at night after I've had a few glasses of wine, the heartbreak convinces me to scroll through the pictures that I can't get myself to delete. Today it decides to strike mid-afternoon.

Swiping through the memories stored on my phone, I watch our story unfold. A blurry shot of the boys sitting on our couch the night we met playing cards. A selfie of Lauren and Graham while Ethan photobombed in the background. The first picture we ever took of just the two of us on my 22nd birthday. It's all here. It's so easy to look back and romanticize the good. The laughs, the kisses, the dates, the road trips. But what about the fights? The screaming, the crying, the nights you slept on the couch. Never documented, hardly discussed. It's like they never existed. It's easy to remember the good moments when they're all we want to see.

On this plane, in the weeds of pictures I wish never existed, something in me finally broke. This wasn't how we were supposed to be. I was supposed to be flying home to him while we were figuring out long distance. Instead, I was consuming him through old memories. I hate that I have to disturb my seat neighbors and excuse myself to the bathroom. I try not to grip the headrests of other people's seats as I make my way to the front of the airplane. I lock myself in the bathroom and lay my head in my hands. Good thing it's a short flight.

~

My alarm goes off at 6 a.m. and I lay there for a few minutes before the day starts. I look around the cold, modern hotel room and try to remember when I used to dream about having a job like mine and traveling on my own. That thought and the craving for a vanilla latte got me out of bed and into the shower. I'm still surprised that Annie chose me to present for her at this year's Boston Writers Workshop but I'm sure it was because my breakup article still holds *The Gist* title for most viewed this year.

There's a Starbucks in the hotel lobby, so I stop there

before I head to the conference. If I weren't running late, I would find a local coffee spot, but this will have to do. Boston in February is even worse than New York, which I didn't know was possible. I can barely feel my hands even with gloves on while holding my hot coffee. Luckily the conference center is only a block away, so I don't have to go too far. I feel my phone ringing in the pocket of my trench coat, so I reach for it.

"Hello?" I answer.

"Morning, baby," Reese says on the other line. "I wasn't sure if I'd catch you. How are you feeling today?"

"I'm good. Pretty nervous, but I'm excited. I've been reciting everything basically since the moment I left the city. I'm running late though and I'm just walking up so I might have to go," I frantically explain.

"I know," he says.

"What do you mean you know?" I adjust the bag on my shoulder and look up to make sure I'm about to enter the right building.

"I'm here," Reese says into the phone as I make eye contact with him. He's standing in the lobby, right in front of me.

"What are you doing here?" I shove my phone into my purse as he embraces me.

"I got on the first flight out this morning. I told my boss I'd work from our Boston office tomorrow and meet some clients for him if he gave me the morning to travel. I have some calls but I blocked my calendar during your session so I could sit in."

"You didn't have to do that."

"I wanted to. I feel bad about the way I handled things last weekend and I know how much this means to you, so

146

I wanted to come and cheer you on. Plus, picturing you giving a presentation on stage turned me on a bit."

"Oh, stop it." I blush. "I have to go check in and prepare. Will you be okay on your own until I'm done?"

"Yeah, I'll work from the coffee shop across the street and make my way back over around 10:30. It'll be about an hour, right? Will you have time to get lunch after? I haven't been to Boston in years, and I have some spots I want to bring you as an early birthday present."

"I'm yours for lunch and dinner." I kiss him on the cheek and head to the front desk.

You know those little moments you long for in relationships? This was one of those. I always wanted someone to surprise me. Whether it was knocking on my door unannounced, sending flowers to my office just because, or showing up at a special event I wasn't expecting them at. Reese showing up makes me feel important.

~

I present Annie's slides, which I helped her create, and make sure to put my own personality into them. In college, I never understood a lot of what was taught to me in class, so I made sure to make the presentation relatable and easy to understand. I used my article "An Open Letter to the Guy I Never Dated" as an example. The reason it gained so much momentum almost overnight was that the title was captivating, readers love a good hook, and it isn't a topic that was often written or talked about. It's the most vulnerable piece of content I've ever written. I walk back into the lobby to find Reese on a bench right outside of the doors.

"Baby, you crushed it." He grabs my face and kisses

me. "Seriously, what a boss."

I'm surprised Reese is so supportive of a piece of content that's about someone he despises.

"Okay, okay. Calm down." I laugh.

"Just saying, I'm proud of you. It's cool to see how passionate you are about work." He nudges me. "Now, let's go get drunk."

"What about your meetings?"

"I pushed them all back. We're here, let's take advantage of it."

I don't consider myself a spontaneous person. I'm a planner and I like to be able to prepare for whatever lies ahead, but something comes over me. Before we find a place for lunch, we drop off his suitcase in my hotel room. We're staying in the Seaport district which is where all of the good bars and restaurants are and it's all walkable, especially once a liquor blanket is established. We get to the door of my hotel room and a wave of spontaneity washes over me. I unlock the door as Reese follows me in and sets his things near the closet. I come up from behind him and wrap my arms around his stomach.

"Someone's in a good mood." He turns around and I stare up at him with a look in my eye that I hope says 'kiss me'. He towers over me and in this moment, I realize that I love how tall he is. His lips come down over mine and I completely lose my train of thought.

Reese gently pushes me up against the wardrobe doors and continues to kiss me but with more force this time. I push against him, and my mouth follows his motions until he pulls away and leads me toward the bed. We simultaneously undress and I motion for Reese to lie on the bed as I make my way on top of him. At this moment,

I need to feel in control.

After, I kiss him and then we lay next to each other breathing heavily in silence. I pick up my pants off the floor and fold them as I try to remember what other clothes that I packed for this trip, so I don't have to wear slacks for the rest of day. I sort through my suitcase and pull out my favorite pair of jeans and a chunky neutral turtleneck— the perfect cold-weather outfit.

"Your phone's been going off." Reese hands it to me as he slides his belt through a loop on the waistband of his navy-colored khakis. I swipe it from him to see I have four missed calls from Lauren.

"What the fuck!" she shouts into the phone.

Reese looks at me with an *are you okay?* expression on his face and I nod as I brace myself for the conversation that I know is about to unfold.

"You saw the post?" I assume.

"You knew? Why didn't you call me? Or even text?"

"I saw it when I was turning my phone on airplane mode and then had two glasses of wine on the flight so by the time, I landed I think I forgot it happened. I'm so sorry, Laur."

"It's fine. I mean, it's not fine but I get it. I can't believe this! They've been dating, what, a little over a year? We're only 23, what's the rush in getting engaged?" she spirals. "Oh my god, do you think she's pregnant?"

"I doubt she's pregnant. I think he's just ready to settle down. Plus, you know his family. They're so by the book that if they can't live together until marriage, this was probably the next step."

"Did you know it was happening?"

"No, I had no idea."

"That makes me feel better." I hear her sigh. I can't imagine how she feels, and I hope I never have to. "How'd today go? When are you coming home? I miss you."

"It was great! I just got back to the room and I'm about to go grab something to eat but I'll be back tomorrow. Let's go out?" I hold off on mentioning Reese surprising me in Boston; it doesn't seem like the right time to bring it up.

"A bestie date? I'm in. I'll make us a res somewhere then we can hit the bars. Love you, hopefully, tonight isn't too miserable. Try somewhere besides the hotel restaurant!"

Lauren knows I hate going out to eat by myself as it just makes me feel so alone. I look across the room at Reese who's patiently waiting for me with no complaints.

"I will. Love you too." I hang up.

"Time for lunch now?" Reese heads for the door. As I follow him down the hall, I can't help but wonder what Ethan thinks about Graham getting engaged. Is he thinking about me, the same way that I'm thinking about him?

~

I get back to the city the next day still not knowing what it's like to travel with a significant other, since Reese stayed in Boston for work. In a way, I'm kind of glad. The Uber driver pulls my suitcase out of the trunk, and I thank him for the ride before greeting Phillip at our door.

"You've got some out-of-town guests this week I hear?" he says.

"Do we?" I reply, wondering if some of Lauren's friends were upstairs pregaming for our night out.

"Have a good one, Sloane." he nods.

I continue through the lobby and up the elevator. As the doors open and I step out of the elevator onto the third floor, I hear loud music and a lot of laughs coming from our side of the hallway. At least Lauren's in a better mood than when I last talked to her. I unlock our front door and see a pair of shoes under our entryway table that I don't recognize.

"I'm home!" I announce myself.

"Is that Sloane?" a familiar voice says from around the corner. It takes me a second to recognize who it is.

"Jordan!" I drop my bags and run into the kitchen. "Holy shit, what are you doing here?"

"Someone had to come to pick up the pieces, am I right?" She motions over toward Lauren as we all laugh. "But also, I'm here for your early birthday celebration!"

"It's a roomie reunion!" Lauren chimes in.

I take off down the hall to get ready and catch up to their level of drunk. In my bedroom, I throw open the suitcase and pull out my favorite pair of jeans that probably need a wash, but I decide they can make it one more night without one. I stare into the small abyss that is my closet and try to decide on a top to wear before I settle on a black bodysuit. Another go-to. I pull the outfit together with a pair of black ankle boots and touch up my makeup before heading back to the kitchen to pregame.

A weekend with Lauren and Jordan both excites and frightens me. I've been trying so hard to move on from the person I was in college. I want to make new memories, fall in love and stop comparing everything back to Ethan. With Jordan here, that feels impossible.

"Are you okay?" Jordan whispers to me.

"Just exhausted from traveling," I lie. "I'm so excited

you're here though!"

"I've missed you guys so much. Wilmington isn't the same without you," she replies.

"Move to the city, J! Haven't you seen those people that fit like five people into a two-bedroom apartment using flex walls? We could totally do that." I can't tell if Lauren's being serious or not.

"Maybe I'll consider it next year. I'd rather not have a flex wall for a bedroom and hear both of you having sex all the time. Speaking of which, Lauren sort of filled me in. Ethan? Living in this building? So bizarre." Jordan turns to me.

I run them both through the awkward elevator encounter between Reese and Ethan, how mad Reese was after, and then his surprising me on my work trip. When I say it aloud, my life doesn't really sound that bad. I'll admit, it isn't. Bad, I mean.

"Second date says that him and some friends will meet us out!" Lauren announces. The look on Jordan's face says she's more than confused. "Anywhere in particular you want to celebrate at, Sloane?"

"Second date is his nickname," I say, while shaking my head no to her question. "He's the only guy in the city that's made it to a second date. What's his real name again?"

"Miles, but let's not get ahead of ourselves."

Jordan and I shoot each other wide eyes and a smile. I have a feeling this was more than a second date to Lauren, and I think Jordan does too.

~

The line at Flying Cock isn't long, so we breeze through. Miles orders a round of tequila shots with orange slices and I can tell why Lauren likes him so much. Not only is he tall, built and good looking but he takes care of her and her friends. To Lauren, that was non-negotiable.

"Let's get another shot." Jordan links her arm with mine and pulls me towards the bar. "What's the deal with Miles' friend?"

"Which one? I don't really know any of them, but I can try to find out," I reply.

"The shorter one," she says. "You don't know them? Haven't you all been out together?"

Have I been a shitty friend to Lauren? I don't know Miles, I wasn't there for her when Graham announced his proposal, and I couldn't even name any of the people she's been spending time with the last few weeks. I've been so caught up in the Ethan and Reese saga that I've been putting everyone else on the back burner. I told myself that once I got into a relationship this was something I'd never do. Yet, I'm doing it.

"Honestly, I haven't spent much time with them. Let's go mingle! We can introduce ourselves and I'm sure Lauren will set you up." Jordan follows as I walk through the crowd.

Three hours, four drinks, and one more shot later I find myself in line for the bathroom checking my phone for any new messages. None. I walk back to the corner where we'd been stationed all night and notice the group has dwindled.

"We're gonna head back to his," Lauren whispers. "I think J is hitting it off with Miles' friend, so we'll offer to take them back with us. Do you want to come?"

"I think I'm good. I'm getting tired so I'll get a ride home and save myself for tomorrow. Brunch?"

"Definitely brunch."

Soon enough, I'm the last person from our group at the bar. I head to the bathroom one last time before walking home. I pull out the pair of gloves I always keep in my coat pocket and shove my hands into them. As I walk down 3rd Ave, I can't help but think about the time Ethan came to visit. He was so overwhelmed by the city, I thought he hated it. Now, he lives here. How is that possible? I know I shouldn't, but I dial his number.

"Hello?" he answers quicker than I expect him to.

"Will you come to my apartment tonight?" I ask without hesitation.

"Your apartment? Are you there right now?" he sounds very sober and very confused.

"Almost. I'm on 3rd and 29th."

"I'm a block away from where you are. I'll meet you."

Within minutes, I'm face to face with Ethan Brady. Unsure what to feel and how to act. My entire body lights up when I see him. How is anyone supposed to compete with this feeling? It's impossible.

"You shouldn't be walking home alone. Where are your friends?" He looks past me to see if he recognizes anyone on the sidewalk.

"They all left before me." I continue walking and he follows.

I pray that he doesn't bring up Reese because I already know what I'm doing is wrong. I don't want to think about hurting him. In this moment, all I want to think about is Ethan. I want to pretend that we're back where we were the night before he got on a flight back to Wilmington. I want to pick up where we left off like we never ended because in my mind, we never really did.

"So, where's your boyfriend?"

There it is.

"He's away for work."

"How'd that get started anyway?" Is Ethan Brady… jealous?

"Do we really have to do this?"

He pauses. "No, I guess we don't."

My anxiety heightens as we approach our building, in fear that Phillip will be internally judging me. Luckily, we enter the lobby and he's nowhere to be found. The tightness in my stomach disappears as we call for the elevator and the doors open immediately. Saved by the bell.

"Yours or mine, Hart?" He looks at me as his fingers move from button four over to button five, wavering until I decide.

"Mine."

Suddenly, we're 21 again in the parking lot of Ascent and Ethan is asking me the same question right before we went home together for the first time. I would give anything to go back and tell them how it all plays out. I'm just not sure that would change anything.

The elevator doors open to the fourth floor, and I feel myself shaking. I remind myself that this is my doing, things are on my terms and I'm in control of this moment— sort of. Ethan Brady still has me wrapped around his finger and I know that he knows it too. I struggle with my key as I unlock the door, hoping he can't tell how nervous I am.

"This layout is different than ours. You guys have a lot more space," he observes.

"I bet they're both the same size; you just got screwed

on living space since you have that third bedroom," I point out. "Want a drink?"

"Whatever you're having." He slips his dirty sneakers off and leans against the kitchen counter.

"Let's go to my room," I suggest. We both know this is wrong, yet he follows me and takes a seat on my bed.

"Going somewhere?" he asks, pointing at the suitcase that's standing upright next to my bedroom door.

"No, I got back from a work trip today."

He doesn't ask any other questions. I know that the reason he doesn't ask is because he doesn't care.

"Can I ask you something?" I push myself back on the bed so that I'm almost laying down and Ethan does the same.

"Is that why you invited me over? To interrogate me?" he laughs. "Ask away."

"Why could you never get there with me?"

He sighs. I'm sure this isn't what he expected when my name popped up on his caller ID after midnight. He probably thought I was booty-calling him. While he wasn't necessarily wrong, this booty call came with stipulations. I need closure before I'm ever going to move on.

"I don't know, Sloane." He only uses my first name when it's a serious conversation. "I can't put it into words. It wasn't about you. It's about me. I just can't get there with anyone. If I could, it would be you."

That's all I need to hear. I turn towards him and place the hand that's not holding my glass of wine on his leg. He takes that as a signal and kisses me.

"I've missed this," he mutters against my mouth and my heart feels like it might explode out of my chest.

"Me too." I used to wonder if I'd ever kiss Ethan again. I can't believe I'm kissing him.

The next thing I know, we're both down to just our underwear. He slips my bra off and tosses it to the floor. I get goosebumps as his fingers run up and down my stomach. I have a brief flash of honesty— I know what I'm doing to Reese is wrong, but this moment with Ethan feels so right.

Afterward, we lay so still. His breaths are heavy and mine are short. I turn my back to him and pull the sheets over my naked body. Within minutes, he molds himself to me, my back curved to his chest.

"Ethan?" I whisper.

"Yeah?"

"I think that maybe I would always let you come back," I say softly. "Not that I would sit around waiting for you, but if you told me that you were ready and wanted me back, I'm not sure there's anything that I wouldn't drop for you."

I've missed being held by him. I've missed the way he smells. I've missed the way he feels. I've missed him. We fall asleep like that and it's like a dream I never want to wake up from.

~

The next morning, I wake with my cheek pressed against Ethan's bare chest, and I lift my head to make sure I didn't drool on him. His light snoring calms me for a second until I remember where we are and that he's not supposed to be here. I shoot up out of bed to put on clothes, throwing his onto the bed in the process.

"Good morning to you, too," he groans.

"Oh, shut it. We both know you need to go," I say

frantically. "Well, first I need to make sure no one's home yet. Jordan might have slept here. I'll be right back."

I throw on a t-shirt before I head out of my room and scope out the situation. I see no purses on the counter or shoes tossed by the front door except Ethan's. That would've been a dead giveaway if they came back here last night.

"Okay, you're good," I yell to him.

"It's just barely 8 and you thought those two would be home already?" He grabs his shoes but doesn't bother putting them on. "Don't you remember what they were like in college?"

"I didn't know if Jordan slept out or not, that's why I was worried," I explain.

"Don't worry so much." He pulls me in for a hug and kisses my forehead. "Bye, Hart."

"Bye," I reply and close the door behind him.

I feel my entire face break out into a smile. I can't help but feel excited and hopeful for another future with Ethan, even after what I just did to Reese. Oh god. Reese.

I find my phone and to my surprise have no missed calls or texts from him. I decide to take a shower and think about how I'm going to handle this. I turn on the water and wait for it to get hot to the touch before I step in. I stand there for a minute and let the scorching water hit my skin before turning down the temperature a bit. A hot shower usually rights all my wrongs. Not this one though.

I don't know what it is about Ethan that makes me toss my morals to the side. We've always had this bond that doesn't quite make sense. I think I've always known, deep down, that we probably don't work out in the end. I still can't help but hope that we do.

Chapter 20

ETHAN · FEBRUARY 2018

It's harsh to say, but I know exactly what I'm doing to Sloane. I know I shouldn't be here— in New York City, in her apartment, in her life. I should leave her alone, but I can't. Well, I can but I don't know that I want to.

I watch her move through the kitchen and pour us each a drink. She's lost weight since last summer, not that she had much to lose but her face is slimmer, and her legs are bonier. I can tell by the way she stumbles into the living room that she drank more than she's let on. I'm not sure exactly how I feel about being around her while she's drunk and vulnerable, but my temptation gives in, and I decide to follow her down the hall and into her bedroom anyway.

Without much pause, she starts hammering me with questions. This is always how it goes when she's drinking.

"Why could you never get there with me?" Her hazel eyes are sad.

I sit in silence for a second and think about how to answer them. I'm struggling with what to say because I want to be honest, but I don't know how. What was the right place or time to tell her my parents were arrested when I was young and by default I grew up with Graham's family? How am I supposed to tell her my family didn't love me enough to stick around? How am I supposed to tell her that I worry I'll leave her one day, just like my parents left me? I wonder what love is like for other people. Is it easy? I know it's not supposed to be this hard.

But all of that feels too personal to say out loud. Instead, I feed her a bunch of bullshit that I know she wants to hear.

"It wasn't about you. It's about me. I just can't get there with anyone. If I could, it would be you." I sugarcoat the truth.

Just like that, she's mine again.

Chapter 21

SLOANE · APRIL 2018

It's been over a month since I slept with Ethan, and I still can't get that night out of my head. I haven't told Reese or Lauren. It's not that I haven't wanted to— I've even tried to a few times, it's just a lot harder than I expected. The thought of disappointing either of them crushes me. I also haven't heard from him, unless you count the two word text he sent me on my birthday. Am I wrong for expecting more?

"Sloane?" Lauren calls out. "Can you and Reese go to dinner tonight?"

"With who?" I emerge from my room.

"Miles snagged us a res at Dante at 9. Can you be there? I thought it was about time we went on a double date with our boyfriends." She smiles.

"Boyfriend, huh?" I raise an eyebrow.

"Finally! Right? I was afraid I would have to follow the three-month rule, but he asked before then. Thank God!"

"Three-month rule?"

"You haven't heard of that? A few podcasts I listen to have covered it. Technically there are two three-month rules. One is that if someone has been pursuing you for three months, that usually means they want to date you. The other three-month rule is that once you're exclusively seeing a guy, you give them three months max to make it official. If they don't, you're out of there."

"Interesting. I like that." The wheels in my mind start turning.

"Sorry, I didn't mean. Well, you know." I know that she's referring to Ethan.

"No, I know you didn't. I like the three-month rule. I think the problem with it is that sometimes when you're three months in, you look at it like 'well I'm already three months in'. You know? That's what I would have said if someone told me that back in college. I would have waited and that's where I fucked up. I waited for him to come around. I waited to see if things would get better. So much waiting. Before I knew it, almost a year had passed, and I was still waiting."

"I know and that's why this is such a great rule. Hopefully, it helps people like you from wasting more of their time on someone who isn't meant to be in their life for more than three months."

"Yeah, hopefully," I reply, knowing that if someone told 21-year-old me how things with Ethan would've played out, I still would've done everything the same.

I'll never regret him.

~

We arrive at Dante and it's exactly like I've been imagining. Checkered tiles line the floors and sage green accents carry throughout the entire space. Tables of friends and lovers laugh over cocktails and appetizers. It might be the only restaurant here that captures the aura of the city and the feeling of living here so perfectly. The host leads us to a table near the window and the couples opt to sit next to each other instead of across. As soon as I browse the cocktail menu, Reese puts his hand on my leg and kisses me on the cheek.

I look up to see if Lauren or Miles are paying attention but they're too enthralled in each other's company. Pointing and giggling at the drink menu while they decide what to try first. Reese has been traveling a lot for work this month, so we haven't spent a lot of time together. Honestly, I've been using it as an excuse to figure out how to tell him about Ethan. I know I need to tell him; we just need to make it through this dinner first.

After we clear our plates, Reese puts his card down to pay the check and I wish I could stop him without making a scene. Not only do I feel guilty about sleeping with Ethan but now I'm lying to his face and letting him foot the bill for an expensive tab. I've never felt worse. We part ways from Lauren and Miles on the sidewalk as Reese and I walk towards his place since it's not far from the restaurant.

"You alright?" he asks as he reaches for my hand and locks his fingers in mine. "You were quiet at dinner."

"Yeah, I'm fine. Just tired." I try to sound convincing.

"I hear that. Miles is cool and seems like Lauren is happy. What do you think of him?"

"I think he's nice and seems to really like her. I just worry they're moving too fast."

"Too fast?" He looks at me. "Haven't they been seeing each other for a few months?"

"Yeah, I don't know, it just feels fast." I can tell he doesn't agree.

We walk the next few blocks hand in hand until we get to Reese's apartment. I don't even want to step foot inside his building, let alone spend the night here. But I also don't want to have this conversation with him. I don't know which option is worse.

"Do you want wine or anything? We could finish that episode of *The Walking Dead* we were watching," he offers.

"Can we just go to bed? I'm exhausted," I ask.

"Yeah, of course." He sets the bottle down. "You're sure you're feeling okay?"

I nod. He follows me into his room and hands me one of his t-shirts to sleep in. I strip out of my jeans, turtleneck, and bra so that I'm only wearing his shirt and my underwear. I slide into his bed and wonder if this is the last time I'll ever be in it. I feel bad that this is how it's ending but no matter how much I've tried to love Reese, it'll never live up to the way that I love Ethan.

"I slept with Ethan."

The words leave my mouth before I even realize what I'm saying. My back is turned and somehow, I find the courage to sit up and make eye contact with him. He stands at the foot of his bed with a blank stare.

"I knew it." I can hear the disappointment in his tone of voice. "I'm not blind, Sloane. I knew this was going to happen, I was just hoping it wouldn't. I was hoping I meant more to you than that."

That one hurts.

"It's not that you don't mean anything to me—"

"I'm not him. No one is and I wish you could realize

that you deserve better than someone who isn't sure about you."

"You don't get it," I reply.

"What don't I get, Sloane? That you would do anything for someone who couldn't give two shits about you? For the last eight months, I've tried to show you the kind of love you deserve but clearly that wasn't enough. You'd rather wait on someone who's hurt you time and time again. You're just as fucked up as him." I feel a tear roll down my cheek and for once, Reese doesn't bat an eye.

"I don't know what else to say. I can't explain it."

I stand up and bring my clothes into the bathroom to change back into because the thought of being naked around him ever again makes my skin crawl. I fold the t-shirt, place it on his dresser and feel him watching my every move.

"I hope you realize it someday," he says. "He'll never change. He's going to hurt you again."

My throat tightens as he continues.

"He's going to hurt you again and this time I'm not going to be there to put you back together."

I leave his apartment without saying another word. The next thing I know, I'm sitting on the front steps of his walkup in the middle of the West Village wondering what to do next. I order an Uber because taking the subway this late alone was one thing I promised my parents I'd never do. I charge the ride to my mom's credit card as I wait for the car to pull up.

As I stare through the window of the black Toyota Camry that smells like cigarettes, I wonder if I'm making the right decision. On paper, Reese is husband material.

He's kind, attentive, reliable, and listens to me— he pays attention and understands what I want and need. That feels like a rare quality to find in a guy these days. I just don't think I'd ever be able to shake the feeling that he isn't the one. Maybe Ethan isn't either. But I sure as hell had to give myself another chance to find out.

I hesitate to get out of the car as it pulls up to my building. I'm alone. Is this a good thing? Or did I just give up the kind of person most women long to spend their life with? What did I just do?

The lobby is completely empty; even Phillip isn't around. I wait for the elevator and hit the button to take me to the fifth floor. I pause at the door of Ethan's apartment. Why did I think this was a good idea? I debate on going back downstairs but knock on the door anyway. Seconds later, he opens it.

"This is a surprise," Ethan greets me. "Everything okay?"

"Can I sleep here tonight?" I cut right to it.

"Yeah, sure. What happened?" He opens the door and motions for me to come inside.

"Do you have anything to drink?" I ask.

"Someone's needy," he laughs. "I always have whiskey. Are you sure that's a good idea though?"

"I don't need a lecture, I'm stone cold sober. I just need a drink and someone to vent to," I argue.

"Alright, I'm listening." He pours us each a glass and sits next to me on the couch.

"I broke up with Reese." I take a sip without recoiling. "Why didn't you text me after we slept together?"

"Well, up until now I thought you had a boyfriend. I already felt shitty enough about what happened. I really didn't want to make it worse."

I don't say anything.

"Did you break up with him because of me?" Ethan asks.

"No." I don't hesitate. "I just knew he wasn't it for me. But if I'm being honest, I don't know that anyone will ever live up to you."

"Don't say that, Sloane, don't put me on some kind of pedestal. I don't deserve it."

"I can't help it. Even before I ran into you again, I kept thinking of how much I missed you. I'm attached to you in this weird way— like our paths were meant to cross and they'll continue side by side until it's time for them to cross again."

"I get that," he says under his breath, as if he doesn't want to admit he feels the same.

Neither of us says anything for a few minutes until Ethan takes my glass and refills them both. When he returns to the couch this time, he sits so close to me that our legs are almost touching. Even after years of knowing him, his body near mine makes me extremely nervous. I swing my legs up so that they're over his thighs and he rests a hand on my knee. We talk about work and life lately. For a second, it feels like we picked up right where we left off.

He leads me into his room. I get under his navy bedsheets, and he pulls me toward him. We don't have sex. Instead we fall asleep with our legs intertwined, my head on his chest and his arms around me. I wish I could fall asleep like this every single night.

~

I sneak back into our apartment the next morning

167

without waking Lauren and Miles. I put on sweatpants and a t-shirt and crawl into bed. Instead of trying to go back to sleep, I open Instagram. Graham and Emily were working on their wedding website, Jordan went to sushi with some of her co-workers and Reese didn't post anything— which isn't out of the ordinary especially considering last night's chain of events, but I type his name into the search bar anyway.

No user found.

Seriously— he blocked me? I toss my phone and pull the covers over me. Maybe I do need a few more hours of sleep before I can face today. After all, I know Lauren isn't going to be ecstatic when I tell her what happened after we left dinner.

~

"You did what?" She stares at me blankly. "Why would you break up with him?"

"I'm gonna… go. I'll text you." Miles kisses Lauren on the cheek and hightails it out of our apartment. I wish I could do the same right now.

"Start from the beginning," she demands.

"The weekend Jordan came to visit, and you guys left the bar, I called Ethan. I was drunk. We slept together and then I didn't talk to him again after that."

"Bullshit."

"Swear. I wanted to tell Reese right after it happened but then he was traveling almost every week for work and the longer I waited, the harder it got. After dinner, I just couldn't keep it in. So, I told him."

"How did he react?" She sips her coffee.

"He said he knew it was going to happen. I mean, he was still pissed, but he wasn't surprised. I don't know if that was necessarily helpful, but I think the fact that it wasn't completely out of nowhere might make it an easier pill to swallow."

"You guys just seemed so... good. Before you knew Ethan was here anyway."

"Maybe that's how I made it seem, but my relationship with Reese was so one-sided. I knew he loved me, and I strung him along because it felt good to feel like someone's everything. He was never my everything though," I explain. "On Valentine's Day, we were at dinner, and I imagined what it would be like if he stood up, walked out of the restaurant and never came back. I would've felt relieved. But with Ethan, I would've felt like someone punched me in the gut repeatedly. From that night on, everything just unraveled."

"So, what's going on with Ethan?"

"I don't know. I've been more honest with him this time around. It hasn't scared him off yet, so I think that's a good sign," I confess.

"Has he changed at all? What would be different this time around?"

"I don't know, yet. It hasn't even been 24 hours since I broke up with Reese."

"Why are you still doing this after all these years?" She seems frustrated. "What is it about him? It's like he has some hold on you or something."

"Sometimes it feels that way. This might sound crazy, but it feels like something is telling me to wait a little more. That one day soon something is going to happen. I know he still thinks about me and has feelings for me, I'm just waiting for him to be ready to act on them."

"That's exactly it. He probably does still have feelings for you but that isn't what matters. What matters is what he's doing about it, which is nothing. If he's doing nothing, you should most certainly be doing the same. Not breaking up with your damn near perfect boyfriend for him. You deserve someone who goes out of their way to make it obvious that they want you in their life."

"If I didn't break up with Reese, I would've been doing the same thing to him that Ethan did to me. It wasn't fair."

"I hope you know what you're doing."

I make my way down the hall, shut my bedroom door, and dial Graham's number. Sometimes I feel like he's the only person who understands my relationship with Ethan. Probably because he's the only person in the world that understands Ethan. I'm jealous of him for that.

"Hey!" he answers.

"Hi, sorry to call so randomly. How's wedding planning going?"

"It's going. What's up? Usually when you call it's with an agenda."

"You make me sound like such a bad friend," I say. "You know how I've been seeing Reese for like a year? Well, I hooked up with Ethan recently and finally told him last night."

"God, Sloane..."

"I broke up with him. I mean, it's what I wanted to do all along, I think. I liked the comfort of him, but I never liked him the same way I like Ethan."

"Can I say something?" he interrupts. "You're never going to like anyone in the way you like Ethan. Honestly, it would be unhealthy if you did. You guys are each other's first loves. No one ever wants to experience that twice because it's usually so toxic."

"We're not toxic," I argue.

"You're missing the point. Did you talk to Ethan? Is he ready for a relationship?"

"Well, no."

"Exactly. So, you're right back at square one. I'm not saying that you shouldn't have broken up with Reese because clearly you didn't want to be with him. But you don't have to go back to Ethan. You can be alone or meet someone else, too. You know that right?"

"I know. But do you think it ever could work out with him?"

"I don't know. Ethan's a hard person to love. He's been through a lot of shit in his life. I don't know if settling down or getting married is something he'll ever want. And you can't wait around forever to find out."

I sigh. He's right.

"Thanks, Graham."

"That's what I'm here for, right?" he laughs. "Save the dates are coming to a mailbox near you. Oh, and Emily and I are planning a trip in the next few months. We'd love to grab dinner."

"Sounds great! Just let me know when and I'll book us a reservation."

I hang up the phone and sigh. I know Graham and Lauren are right. If I start hanging out with Ethan again, I need to lay down some ground rules. He needs to be all in. I just don't know that I have the courage to tell him that.

Chapter 22

SLOANE · JUNE 2018

I've missed having sex with Ethan. Before him, sex was nothing but a way to gain validation and attention from men. The chemistry between us is unlike anything else I'd ever experienced, and the sex is even better. Maybe I like having sex with him so much because that's the only time he really let his walls down. It's the only time I truly feel like we're on a level playing field.

"Will you get a towel?" I ask.

"Yep, got it," Ethan mumbles.

After I broke up with Reese, Ethan and I picked up where we left off a year ago. We haven't talked about what we are or what either of us wants, and I'm okay with that if it means that he's back in my life. He hands me a towel and makes his way back under the sheets before turning on my TV.

Bzzz. Bzzz. Bzzz. His phone lies face down on his stomach as he lets it ring.

"Aren't you going to see who it is?" I ask.

He turns it over so that we can both see it's an

unknown number with a Wilmington area code. He turns the phone back over and keeps flipping through Netflix to find something for us to watch.

"You don't want to answer?" I ask again.

"It's probably just spam." he replies, unphased.

I let it go and lay my head on his chest. He decides on our favorite season of *Breaking Bad* and turns off the lamp beside him so that the only thing lighting up the room is the glow from my 32-inch flat screen. I tilt my head up to look at him because sometimes small moments like these don't feel real. I used to lay in this bed longing for him and now he's back like he never left. He smiles and strokes my hair as I fall asleep on him.

~

"Alright, so Graham gets into town around 2. He said they're going to check into their hotel and then get us a table at some rooftop Emily's been dying to try," Ethan says with a mouth full of toothpaste.

"Did he say which one? We probably need a res. It's a Friday," I suggest as I hurriedly pack my bag for work and find a pair of shoes that will go well from day to night.

"Not sure. That's why they're going to try and get there before 5. Think you can leave early today?" he asks.

I'm so envious of his job sometimes. Men have it so easy. On Fridays, his team goes out to lunch and never goes back to the office. They have what his boss calls 'brainstorm beers' and then call it a day.

"I can try. I wanted to come back here to change but maybe I'll just throw an extra outfit into my bag."

"Why change? You look great."

Ethan comes up behind me as I'm looking at myself in my mirrored closet doors. I chose a light blue mini dress with tiny, embroidered flowers paired with an oversized white blazer because the office is always freezing. I just had to decide between white ankle boots or sneakers.

"Go with the sneakers. Casual Friday," he whispers in my ear and proceeds to grab me by the waist and kiss my neck.

"Okay fine, they're easier to travel in anyway." I turn around and kiss him back. "I'm about to be late."

"It'll be worth it." I can feel him as he presses up against me.

"Seriously, Ethan," I plead. "It's not the morning for this."

Something about Ethan in a button-down and slacks turns me on. I kiss him goodbye and leave him to finish getting ready in my apartment. I got him a copy of our key about a month after we started consistently seeing each other again. Lauren wasn't a huge fan of the idea, but she didn't say no either. She's been spending so much time at Miles', it's like she lives there now.

I get to work early in hopes that I'm able to leave early. No one ever shows up before 8:30 am on Fridays because Thursdays are infamously late nights. My cube is so full of sticky notes with deadlines and reminders that they might as well be considered decor. I clean some of them up and get to work on new pieces.

"Gem tonight?" Mila sits down in her cube across from mine.

"Our college friends are coming into town today and they're wanting to find a rooftop, but I'm definitely going to try and convince them to hit Gem after," I reply, still typing away.

"Sloane?" Annie calls from her office.

I stop what I'm working on and take my laptop to her office. A knot starts to form in both my stomach and throat.

"Sit." She motions toward the chair in front of her. "So, you've single-handedly generated our website fifteen million views this month. The board, and I, of course, want to promote you to Senior Staff Writer."

"Really?" I'm stunned.

"You've been doing great. Your work has been resonating with our audience, you've been stepping in for me and you've been such a team player. You deserve this." She smiles.

"I don't know what to say," I reply. "Thank you!"

"Of course. Now, get out of here. Start your weekend early and go celebrate." She waves me off.

I return to my desk and tie up a few loose ends before checking the time. I pack up my things and decide to make a pit stop to drop off my work bag and potentially do a quick outfit change. I text Ethan on my way to the subway and debate on calling my parents to tell them, wondering if either of them would even answer. Before I'm able to hit dial, I feel my phone vibrate in my hand.

Ethan Brady: Leaving Flying Cock now, Graham is heading to Mr. Purple. Emily is insisting. Meet us?
Me: *eye roll* See you soon ;)

I hit send as I head down the steps into the subway to take the next train to the Lower East Side. According to every New Yorker I've ever met, Mr. Purple was only decent the first few months after it opened. No one really goes there anymore, mostly because of all the tourists. But as a former tourist, I see why she wants to go.

"Sloane!" Emily waves me down from across the roof.

"Hi, guys!" I say as I approach the table.

"It's so nice to finally meet you!" She immediately embraces me in a hug.

Emily is a breath of fresh air, much more Graham's speed than Lauren was. No offense, Laur. She has beautiful long brown hair and a smile that seems like it never leaves her face. From what I've heard from Graham, Emily is kind, genuine, and always makes him laugh. Even though I've only known her for a few minutes, I can tell right away they're meant for each other.

"Whatcha want to drink?" Ethan asks me.

"Get the blackberry mojito! They're so good!" Emily chimes in.

"I'll have that." I smile and watch him walk to the bar. "So, how've you guys been?"

"Oh my gosh, you wouldn't believe how intense wedding planning is. It's like one thing after another. Don't even get me started on the seating chart. It's a shit show." Emily laughs.

"What about you?" Graham interrupts before we get in so deep with the wedding talk that we can't get out.

"Actually." I pause until Ethan reaches the table with my drink. "I got a promotion today! You're looking at *The Gist*'s newest Senior Staff Writer."

"I'm so proud of you," he whispers in my ear.

Success feels great, but his affirmation makes me feel better. Ethan puts his arm around me as the table echoes congratulations and Graham orders us a round of celebratory shots.

"Lauren's calling me." I look down at my phone. And

step away from the table. "Hey!"

"Hey, where are you?"

Shit. I never got the chance to tell her that Graham was coming to town this weekend. "Are you working late? I wanna go out!"

"Don't hate me… I totally forgot to mention Graham is here this weekend. I'm out with him and Ethan."

"Is Emily there? Would it be weird if I came? I'm not trying to stay in tonight."

"She's here, but I think it would be fine. Is Miles around? Not sure if that would make things more awkward or less."

"I'm sure I can convince him. Where are you?"

"Mr. Purple." I laugh.

"You're shitting me." She laughs. "We can be there in twenty."

Walking back to the table, I think through the best way to tell everyone Lauren and her boyfriend are on the way. After we moved to the city, Graham stopped mentioning her, as did she, until he got engaged anyway. Now that she has Miles, I think she's feeling less jealous.

"Lauren's coming with her boyfriend, is that okay?"

"Yeah, all good. I'm happy for her. Is he a good guy?"

"He is."

"That's all I need to hear."

After a few awkward introductions and another round of drinks, we decide to get dinner before going to Gem. Two blocks away is one of the best Mexican restaurants in the city, according to Miles. We order a round of margaritas, tequila shots, queso, and guac before putting in our entrees. By the time we're ready to leave, I'm more than tipsy but the night is young, so I try and pull myself together.

"Fuck this line," Lauren complains.

"It's not that bad," Graham argues back.

Ethan and I shoot each other a look while keeping both of our mouths shut. I peer inside the window and that's when I spot Reese.

"We could always try Flying Cock?" I offer, hoping someone would take the bait.

"It's too low-key. Let's go there after this," Ethan replies.

Once we make it inside, we're body to body. I grab Ethan's hand and follow him to the bar where he orders everyone's first round of drinks. As we wiggle our way back into the sea of people, Ethan bumps into Reese. They both nod as if to acknowledge each other's existence, but Reese avoids any eye contact with me.

"Let's dance!"

Lauren grabs me by the hand and leads me through the crowd while the DJ plays a mash-up of Travis Scott, Drake, and Post Malone.

"Are you okay?" she asks when we find a spot on the edge of the dance floor. "I saw Reese."

"Yeah, I'm okay. I just hate that I hurt him."

As the rest of the group approaches, we change the subject. Ethan comes up from behind me and I can tell he's buzzed. He starts swaying my body to the music and makes me forget about Reese.

Chapter 23

ETHAN · JULY 2018

Living in New York City is exhausting— ten-hour days in the office, followed by happy hours, followed by sleepovers with Sloane doesn't leave a lot of time for myself. I used to go to the gym every day; now I'm lucky if I get there once a week. I can see a difference in myself. My face has gained a little bit of weight and I've lost definition in my chest, abs and arms.

Things with Sloane have been surprisingly good. We still haven't established any sort of title, but with the amount of time we're spending together, I'd say we're pretty much a couple. I know she avoids asking what we are because of everything that happened in college and that's been more than okay with me. Something about not having a title makes me feel less pressure. I text her as I'm leaving the office to let her know I'm hitting the gym and then I'll come over.

The gym is packed, and I wonder why I pay almost $200 a month to not even find a machine. Coming here is supposed to clear my head, not make me more stressed.

After an hour of hitting weights, I sit in the sauna and lean my head back against the wood planks. I forgot how much I missed this uninterrupted time. No phone, no people, no thoughts. I close my eyes and stay in there until I feel like I'm going to pass out, grab my backpack from the locker and take the subway home.

"Hey!" Sloane greets me from the kitchen before I can even close the door behind me. "Noah let me in. Lauren and Miles are cooking at my place, so I figured I'd bring food over here, so you didn't have to worry about cooking. I know it's been a long day."

Not only am I slightly annoyed that she invited herself over but also that she's here in general. I just got done sweating my ass off at the gym and in air condition-less subway— I was looking forward to a quiet apartment and an ice-cold shower. I force a smile as I walk into the kitchen.

"Thanks, you didn't have to do this," I say. "I'm all sweaty so I'm gonna shower before I eat. You can start though."

I continue to the bathroom without turning back to look at Sloane because I know I'll see the disappointment in her face. She means well, and I appreciate the effort, but sometimes it's just too much. I take an extra-long shower to try and bring my mood back up, but I still feel just as shitty afterwards. I throw on a pair of boxers and basketball shorts before making my way back into the common area where Sloane is waiting for me.

"Do you want me to leave?" she asks. "I'm sorry. I should've texted before coming."

"No, no, it's fine. I'm sorry I'm just tired," I lie. I pull her into a hug and rest my chin on the top of her head.

Sometimes I forget how short she is.

"Okay… If you're sure. Want me to heat up your food?"

"That'd be great. I'll find something for us to watch." I kiss her and then get comfortable on the couch. I feel bad for being standoff-ish earlier.

Minutes later she hands me a microwaved bowl of hibachi chicken and rice then sits on the side of the couch opposite from me. I can tell she's a little upset by my attitude earlier, but I try not to think too much about it. We watch a new movie that's in Netflix's top ten. By the time it's over, I notice Sloane's drank over half a bottle of wine by herself. With wine usually comes a fight or a game of 20 questions, but before she has the chance to start either, I start kissing her. I pick her up off the couch and kiss her the entire way to my bedroom where I take off her clothes and stare at her in the glow of the streetlights. Sloane falls back on her elbows and even though I can't see it, I know she's blushing.

She's lying on her back as I'm on top of her, and in between breaths and moans, she says it— the words I've been dreading to hear.

"I love—" She stops once she realizes what she's about to say. "Fucking you."

I immediately bring her mouth into mine to avoid any further conversation until I've finished. We remain quietly in our positions for a few seconds before I excuse myself to the bathroom.

When I come back, she's laying in one of my t-shirts on the far side of the bed with her back facing me. I climb into bed and bring my body closer to hers. I can tell she's upset with me, but instead of addressing it, I lay behind her until she falls asleep. Then I turn over and scroll on my phone for a while until my eyes start to get heavy.

What have I gotten myself into?

Chapter 24

SLOANE · SEPTEMBER 2018

Suddenly, the seasons have changed. Fall in New York is a different kind of serotonin rush. It reminds me exactly why I moved here and what this city is capable of. The crisp air, burnt orange leaves, rainy days and cooler temperatures bring out a different side of New Yorkers. I swear, people only smile at me on the subway between the months of September through December.

I decide to take myself shopping after work today because I need jackets and a new pair of jeans. Well, I don't need them, but I want them. I stroll down Park Avenue, where I'd kill to have an apartment one day; it's everyone's dream. I stop into a few stores before deciding on a new leather jacket and a pair of mom jeans, which are apparently beginning to come back this year. After spending what felt like was half of my paycheck, I call Lauren on my walk to the subway to see if she wants to meet for a drink.

"Drinks?" I ask as soon as she picks up the phone.

"Oh my gosh, yes! I could use apps too." She laughs.

"Can you get there soon? I'm already in midtown so I shouldn't be more than 20."

"On my way."

It's early and the restaurant is nearly empty, so I snag us seats at the bar and order two extra dirty martinis, Lauren's favorite.

"Martinis on a Wednesday?" She sneaks up behind me. "What's the occasion?"

"Just some light roommate bonding. I feel like we haven't spent a lot of time together lately," I reply. "I hate it."

"I know, babe, me too. The boys are getting in our way!" She laughs and lifts her glass, then we take our first sip.

"So how are things with Miles?" I ask.

"He's great, Sloane. Really like the best person I've ever met— besides you, of course," she catches herself. "I see a future with him, A really good future."

"I'm so happy for you!" I take another sip.

"How about Ethan? How's that going? You seem to be spending a lot of time together so that's good! Right?" She looks at me skeptically.

"Things are good!" I lie. "Same old, same old."

Three martinis later and we can't stop laughing. Every other sentence that comes out of our mouths make us laugh harder than the last. Lauren's phone starts vibrating on the bar, and I motion for her to answer it. I can see it's Miles.

"Hey!" she says. "I'm with Sloane getting drinks. Yeah, we'll probably get checks soon, we've had three already. Okay that works. I'll meet you outside of our place. Love you too."

They say I love you already? I mentally count the months they've been together in my head. Well, I guess it's been about six. Do six short months warrant "I love you's"?

"I'm gonna come home with you since we've both had a few drinks and then Miles is going to take an Uber to come and get me."

"That's really nice of him."

When we get home, Miles is waiting outside for Lauren. They come upstairs for a few minutes so she can pack a bag with a change of clothes while I go into my room to call Ethan.

"Hey," he answers. "Everything okay?"

"Yes, does something have to be wrong for me to call?" I ask hastily.

"I didn't mean it like that. What's up?"

"Can you sleep here tonight?"

"Not tonight," he replies as I sigh into the phone. "Tomorrow? There's a game on. We can watch it together and order in. I'll even bring wine."

"Fine," I groan.

"Get some sleep, drunkie. Good night." He laughs.

"Night." I hang up.

~

The next night Ethan shows up at my apartment with two pizzas and a bottle of Cab. After we eat, he sits on the couch and his eyes are glued to the Patriots game while I send through a pitch for work. These everyday moments with him still feel somewhat surreal. I hope this is what I'm doing when I'm 50. Is it crazy that I long for a future with him even though we don't have a solid present?

"Your phone is going off." I nod toward the coffee

table and watch as Ethan picks it up and immediately sets it back down again.

"Spam," he replies.

For the past few months, I've noticed that he's been getting phone calls from the same number. I'm not sure if he knows that I've picked up on it, but I have. He passes it off as spam or wrong caller any time I address it, but I can't tell if he truly believes that. The logical part of my brain says that he's lying, and the emotional part says maybe there's more to the story than I want to know.

What if there's another girl?

I can't shake the feeling that it's a possibility, but I'll continue to ignore it for a little while longer if it means not losing Ethan. In the same moment, mid-thought, my phone rings.

"Hey, Mom." I pick up and walk into my bedroom. "What's up?"

"Do you have Thanksgiving plans yet? We're thinking of going to London for a few weeks and, well, it overlaps with Thanksgiving. I don't want to leave you but..." she rambles on.

"Go, go! I haven't thought about Thanksgiving yet but worse case I can go see Dad. I've always wanted to go to London."

"Me too," she says. "You're sure, honey?"

"I'm sure. Love you, Mom."

"Love you too." She hangs up.

I sit back on the couch, closer to Ethan this time. He puts his arm around me and lays my head on his shoulder. I wish I could stay in this moment forever.

"What're you doing for Thanksgiving?" I ask, partially afraid of the answer.

"Not sure," Ethan says. "Why?"

"My mom's going to London. I guess I can call my dad, but I don't know…" I ramble.

"I'm sure I'll be in the city, so we could just do this?" he offers. "Order take out and watch something."

"That'd be nice."

Finally. He's choosing me.

~

I arrive to work the next morning early because I have a deadline today on an assignment that I've been putting off all week: Do half of all marriages really end in divorce? I interviewed six people, some married, some divorced, some had parents who stayed together until they passed, and some had parents who split before they were even born. The interviews were harder on me than I expected, so I took a week-long break from writing and now I only have nine hours to finish it. I open my laptop, pull up the document and read what I have written so far.

Being married to the love of your life must really be something. Waking up and falling asleep next to your soulmate sounds like the perfect start and end to each day. I imagine your conflicts seem less earth-shattering when you have someone to overcome them with. I hope everyone gets to experience that kind of love one day. Including me.

"My wife and I have been together for 10 years, married for six, and I still get excited to see her every single day when I get home from work. She makes even the worst days bearable, just by existing."

I shut my laptop and put my head in my hands. Why did I pitch this topic? Not only does it break my heart all

187

over again thinking about how one day my parents almost perfect marriage disappeared into thin air, but it makes me question a future between me and Ethan.

One day, five years from now, if he were stopped on the street and asked to talk about the love of his life, what would he say? Presuming he was thinking about me, of course. Would he say that he's never met anyone like me? That I make him feel like a different, better, version of himself? That he feels safe when he's with me? I wonder if he'll ever love me the way I love him. I wonder if he's even capable of a love that deep.

The clock on my phone reads 7:18 p.m. when I finally submit the piece for final review and pack up my things. The office is dead, cubes are empty, and I can hear a vacuum humming down the hall. I hope I'm never the last one to leave again. It's nothing like TV shows make it out to be. I feel less like a girl boss and more like a potential murder victim. As I hurry out of the building, my phone vibrates in my bag. I dig through to find it, and when I do, I see Lauren's name on the screen.

"Hey, sorry just getting out of work," I answer.

"I figured. I just got home with sushi and wine. See you in 20?"

"See you in 20," I assure her.

"You're home!" Lauren yells from the kitchen.

"Finally." I laugh as I take off my shoes and set my work bag down at the door.

She set the counter with two glasses of red and four different kinds of sushi rolls from our favorite Japanese place in the city.

"What's the occasion?" I say before sitting down. I can tell something's up.

"Oh, just sit," she replies. I obey and take a sip of my wine, afraid of what is about to come.

"Are you leaving New York?" I blurt out.

"No, oh my god. Just the apartment. Miles wants me to move in with him. I know it's soon, but I really want to. I spend almost every night there anyway, so it makes sense but that's not the only reason why I want to. I love him, Sloane. Like really, really love him. I think he's it for me."

I take another sip of my wine and digest the news.

"I'm happy for you. Seriously." I grab her hand to let her know that I'm being genuine.

"Oh, fuck off," she laughs. "What is it?"

"No, really, I'm happy for you! I'm just going to miss you. The past two years have gone by so fast, and I think, thanks to *Sex and the City,* I had this preconceived notion that we'd be living together until our 30s."

"I get that, I did too. I didn't think I'd meet someone this fast. Or at all, really."

"So, when are you thinking of moving out?" I ask.

"Well, our lease is up at the end of December so probably around then. I wanted to tell you as soon as I gave him an answer, so you could either find someone to move in or start looking for your own place depending on what you decide."

We ate all four rolls and finished a bottle and a half of wine while we recapped some of our favorite college memories. Even though she wasn't moving out for three months, it felt like I was losing her tomorrow.

"Is it okay if Miles comes over?" Lauren slurs.

"Yeah, I'm going to Ethan's." I giggle.

We're both tipsy and can't stop laughing. I wish

college us would be able to see us now. Living in New York, happy, successful, in love. These were dreams I could've only hoped to achieve one day, and I did in the matter of years.

I knock on Ethan's door, only he's expecting me this time. He answers and greets me with a hug and leads me to his room. I pass his roommates who are playing video games on the couch and don't acknowledge my existence. I ignore it but make a mental note to bring it up to him later.

"Hey." He starts kissing me.

"Hi." I pull away.

"What's wrong?" He sits on the bed and motions for me to join him.

"Lauren told me she's moving in with Miles."

"Shit. When?"

"Our lease ends in January, so around then I guess. I just feel like it's so soon. I'm happy for her, but I'm scared for me."

"What do you mean?"

"I mean, we moved here together; this was our idea. Now it's just me. I've never lived alone or even thought about it. Would I like it? I feel like I'd go crazy." I feel myself start to spiral.

"Calm down." He puts his hand on my leg. "You'll figure it out, Sloane, you always do."

I want to find that reply comforting, but I don't. I take off my leggings so that I'm just in a t-shirt and underwear and climb under his sheets. I can tell they haven't been washed in a few weeks.

"You're gonna be fine without Lauren, you know that, right? She'll just be right down the street," Ethan tries to reassure me.

I pause for a minute.

"Do you think we'll live together one day?" I ask.

He sighs.

"I don't know, Sloane. I can't think about that right now."

I turn over so that I'm no longer facing him and feel myself start to cry. I try to hide the tears, but he notices and wraps me up in his arms. Somehow, even though he's the one that's making me feel bad, he's also the only one who can make me feel better.

Chapter 25

ETHAN · OCTOBER 2018

I stare at my phone as it rings in my hand, even though it's an unknown number. I know exactly who it is on the other side of the call. I just can't bring myself to answer. I take a seat on the edge of my bed and stare at the screen until the call gets sent to voicemail. I've accumulated over 11 new messages that I'll never listen to over the past few months, and I constantly wonder when it'll end.

In June, Mrs. Clark called to let me know my dad was being released from prison. She and Mr. Clark seemed to think he'd show up at their front door asking to speak to me, but after what my mom did, or didn't do rather, I highly doubted that. A month later they called to say he was at their house, and I let them give him my number, never expecting him to call and not knowing if I would answer if he did.

Noah and Lucas are traveling for work this week and Sloane is getting drinks with Lauren, so I have the night to myself which is a nice change of pace. I find the bong and put on the Thursday night football game. Every few minutes I glance over at my phone that sits face down next to me on the leather couch, and after a few bong rips, I finally pick it up. I hesitate before clicking the first voicemail I received and bring the phone to my ear.

"Ethan it's your, um, dad— if I can even call myself that. I've been trying to get ahold of you, and I know you've been ignoring my calls, but I'd really like to talk to you. The Clarks said you're in New York now. I never pictured you as a city boy but then again, I don't know the adult you. Anyway, I hope you're taking care of yourself. Call me back if you can. Okay, well bye."

Instead of chucking the phone across the room like I expected to, I listen to the next voicemail. Then the next, and the next until I reach the one he left tonight. I pace around our living room and debate on what to do next. Do I call him? What could he possibly have to say?

I'm sorry I fucked up your life?

I'm sorry I stopped calling?

I'm sorry your mom never came back for you?

I hold my head in my hands and close my eyes before making my decision. I scroll through my call log until I find Graham's name and I hit it.

"Hey Brady, surprised you're not out tonight," he answers.

"Needed a night in. Do you have a few minutes to talk?" I ask.

"Yeah, of course, what's up? Sounds serious."

"My dad's been calling."

"Fuck. What about?"

"That's just it, I don't know. He says he really needs to talk to me, and I just can't decide if I should call him back. Have your parents mentioned anything to you?"

"They told me that he was getting out of jail a few months ago. What are you gonna do?"

"I don't know, man."

"If you're asking me, I think you should call him back. I know they both really fucked you over and it's okay to never forgive them, but maybe talking to him will help. Maybe hearing exactly what happened or why he stopped calling will help."

"Yeah, maybe." I sigh.

"How are things with Sloane?" he asks.

"They're good," I reply.

"Uh huh." Graham doesn't believe it. "Just know if you keep this shit up for much longer, you're gonna lose her for good, and from what I can tell, you really do like and care about her. A girl like Sloane won't wait around forever."

"Alright, alright." I hang up the phone and set it on the coffee table before taking another hit.

Am I ready to unearth something that happened over 10 years ago? I just want to forget it ever happened and it feels like a phone call with my dad would do the exact opposite of that. I decide to sleep on it— I don't need to decide right this second, so why am I acting like I do?

I text Sloane and tell her the door's unlocked because I don't want to sleep alone tonight, and less than 15 minutes later, she's curled up next to me. Sometimes I don't realize how much I need her.

Chapter 26

SLOANE · NOVEMBER 2018

"Just take the train in and out tomorrow. I don't want you to be alone for Thanksgiving! Miles' mom invited you. They have more than enough food." Lauren zips her suitcase as I lay on her bed.

Last week, exactly ten days before Thanksgiving, Ethan told me that he made plans to go to Wilmington. He didn't ask if I wanted to come, and I guess I didn't expect him to, but that didn't make it hurt any less. It was official: I'd be spending Thanksgiving alone.

"It's fine, really! It'll be nice to have a day to myself. I thought about trying to go to the parade but some of my co-workers said they get there before 5 a.m. which is a huge no from me." I laugh.

"Next year, you should have one of your parents come and maybe mine will and we can all do the parade!" she offers. "I've always wanted to go!"

Lauren's heading to Connecticut to meet Miles' parents for the first time, and as nice as it was for them to extend an invitation, that sounded like the last plan I wanted to crash. The good part about being in the city for Thanksgiving is that nothing really closes, so my take-out options are endless.

"So, what do you think you'll do tomorrow then?"

"*Sex and the City* re-runs and an entire bottle of wine probably," I say, and we both laugh. Lauren lays next to me as she waits for Miles to get here.

"This reminds me of college," she says. "Remember when we'd lay in each other's beds for hours without saying anything? Scrolling Instagram and playing Candy Crush."

"I'm gonna miss living together," I admit.

"Me too."

This is probably the most intimate moment we've ever had. Our friendship is deep, but it's never been too emotional. That's the beauty of Lauren, she keeps life so lighthearted. This moment was different. I could feel our friendship start to shift. It made me scared for the future and made me wonder if I needed to take my relationship with Ethan more seriously. While I hate the thought of having that conversation with him, I hate the thought of being single while all my friends are in love, getting married, and having kids.

With Ethan, there will be more than just one Thanksgiving alone. There will be weddings with no plus one and office holiday parties where I'll get asked where my boyfriend is or if I'm single. I remember the days I used to love being single. I think I could get there again. It's not the thought of being alone that scares me; it's the thought of losing the only person I've ever really loved for good. I loved Reese, but not like this. Loving Ethan is hard to put into words. It's a feeling of comfort and familiarity that I'm so worried I'll never experience again. Maybe that's why I can't let go.

~

The TV asks if I'm still watching as I grab the remote to start the fourth *Sex and the City* episode of the night. Before I hit yes, I scroll Instagram and then Snapchat to see if Graham or Ethan have posted anything. Odds are they're either downtown or at the beach bars. It's Thanksgiving Eve, in their hometown, after all. My anxiety gets the best of me, so I go to the kitchen to pour myself another glass of wine. I empty the bottle into my glass and toss the remnants into the trash can. I sit back on my favorite side of the couch and decide to turn on the movie instead of the show. Every time I watch the scene where Mr. Big leaves Carrie at the altar I cry. And right now, I'm feeling a good cry.

I sip my last glass of wine as I watch a fictional character go through something I'm so afraid of. If I'm terrified of it, why does a small part of me still imagine it happening between me and Ethan? Why do I want to be with someone who I think would leave me at the altar? Even the smallest inkling of that feeling should tell someone that's not who they're meant to end up with. So why am I still with him?

"Sometimes love stories aren't epic novels. Some are short stories, but that doesn't make them any less filled with love," Carrie says.

Tears stream down my face. Is Ethan my Mr. Big? I've always hated Big, but this scene just instilled what I've been contemplating for the past few weeks. I'm so afraid to leave Ethan, even though I know it's the right thing to do. I can't keep waiting around for someone to love me who doesn't. Maybe he does love me. It's not enough though. I leave my empty wine glass on the coffee table and stumble down the hall to my room. Usually, I hate pity parties, but I can't help but feel a little sorry for myself tonight. I'm spending Thanksgiving alone in my small New York City apartment while two of my favorite people are in our college town, without me. Ethan probably doesn't even realize how fucked up it is that he left me here. But it is. It's really fucked up.

Maybe he doesn't know what it's like to have someone who wants to love him, someone who doesn't want to leave him. But that doesn't give him an excuse to treat me as if I don't exist.

~

On Thanksgiving, I wake up with a slight headache and no missed calls or texts. I groan at the fact that I don't have a TV in my room and stumble into the living room to turn on the parade and call my mom.

"Hi honey, happy Thanksgiving!"

"Hey, Mom. Happy Thanksgiving to you too!"

"Are you at the parade?" she asks.

"No, I just woke up."

"Well, your doorman should have some champagne for you. From us. Love you. Can't wait to see you soon!"

"You too, Mom." I hang up.

My favorite bagel place is closed today, so I grab a granola bar from the cabinet and make a cup of coffee. I promised myself I wouldn't start drinking until at least 11 am. My phone buzzes in my hand. Expecting it to be a group chat, I'm pleasantly surprised when I see Ethan's name pop up.

Ethan Brady: Happy Thanksgiving, turkey.

For the next few seconds, I uncontrollably smile at the message.

Chapter 27

ETHAN · NOVEMBER 2018

I hate airports and I hate flying. I don't get how people could possibly enjoy it. Everyone's in a rush, my flight almost always gets delayed for no reason, and I usually end up sitting in front of a kid who kicks my seat the entire trip. This flight was no different. I wait for the passengers in around me to make their way up the aisle, throw my duffle bag over my shoulder and follow them. Luckily, Graham's picking me up which means we'll get a drink before going to his house. God knows I need a few.

"Where's the suit?"

Graham is waiting for me in his top-less Jeep Wrangler. It's an unusually warm day for late November, but that's North Carolina for you, always unpredictable.

"I thought city boys only wore suits everywhere. At least that's what they make it seem like in the movies," he continues.

"Who in their right mind would wear a suit on a flight that cost $80 round trip?"

"Dockside?" Graham asks. "I figured we could sit

outside and get a bucket of beers before seeing the 'rents."

"Thought you'd never ask." I turn up the volume and we listen to "Stir Fry" by Migos followed by a few other songs from that album until we pull into the restaurant parking lot.

"Does it feel good to be back?"

"I haven't been gone that long."

"Dude, it's almost been a year."

Shit, he's right. January marks one year since I packed up, left Wilmington and moved to a city I thought I hated.

"It's gone by so fast." I follow him to the outdoor bar where we take a seat and order a bucket of Corona. The air smells salty and reminds me how much I miss living near the ocean.

"So how are things? Where's Sloane going for Thanksgiving?"

I could've called it. It didn't even take Graham a full hour to bring her up. This happens whenever I go somewhere without her. It's like we're a package deal. What's the point of not being in a relationship if anyone just assumes we are anyway? I'm getting tired of people caring about us more than they care about me. Is that selfish? Maybe. Do I care? No.

"Can we talk about something else? Sometimes it feels like every conversation I have these days seems to revolve around Sloane." I sip my beer. "How are you?"

"Sorry dude, didn't mean anything by it. I'm good. Living at home is getting old though. I wish I could speed up the wedding so Emily and I could live together already. Her parents are so traditional, it hurts."

"Have you looked at new places?"

"We have a two-bedroom apartment over in Mayfaire,

but it's just her living there until the wedding. I stay overnight a lot though— crazy I know. We'll probably live there a year or two and then look at houses."

"Congrats, man."

We finish the bucket of beers and then head to his parents' house. I already know this is going to be a long weekend.

~

"You're sure that you don't want to come out with us?" Graham asks one last time before getting out of the car.

"Maybe later. I'll let you know. Thanks again for letting me borrow your car," I reply.

"Anytime. Just meet or pick us up later. Good luck." He slams the passenger door and I watch as he and Emily walk into the bar hand in hand.

I type the address to a motel twenty minutes outside of Wilmington into my maps app and then turn up the volume on the radio so that I don't have to hear my own thoughts. When I get to the motel, I debate on turning around, but instead I pull into the parking lot and sit in my car for another few minutes before getting out of it. I scan the numbers on the doors until I see 105 and hesitate before knocking.

When the door opens, I'm shocked. I don't know what I expected my dad to look like after ten years in prison, but for some reason I thought he'd be the same guy I remembered. In some ways he is, but he's older and smaller than before.

"Look at you," he says.

I stand in the doorway, still taking in the sight of him. I manage a half smile before he brings me in for a hug. I pat his back and awkwardly wait for him to pull away.

This is so much worse than I expected.

I can tell that he's been drinking but I reluctantly agree to go to dinner with him anyway. Growing up, I never thought of my parents as alcoholics. They owned a bar, so I thought drinking was a part of their job, or at least my dad's, anyway. It wasn't until I was older that I understood he had an issue.

He gets into Graham's car, and I drive us to a restaurant a few minutes away from the motel. The car ride is mostly silent, but my brain won't shut off. I can't believe the guy in the passenger seat is the same guy that raised me. The guy that I called Dad, who taught me how to throw a football and ride a bike. He's a sliver of the guy I remember and is now an ex-con with grey hair, a sunken face full of wrinkles.

We sit across the table from each other, and he orders us two Miller Lites. His fingers drum the neck of the bottle before he asks me the question I've been dreading.

"Have you talked to her? Your mom?"

"Not since she got out. Have you?" I take a big swig of beer.

"The number I had for her has been disconnected for years. I was hoping you had a new one," he says before realizing what I just said. "Did you say that haven't talked to her since she was released?"

"That's exactly what I said."

"She was supposed to go back for you. That was our agreement."

"Well, she didn't. According to Facebook she moved to Texas, got re-married and has a young daughter now."

"Fuck." He rubs his temple before taking another sip of beer. "Fuck her. So, you were living with the Clarks this entire time?"

"Yep."

"They're good people. Real good people."

"So, what was so important that you needed to talk to me after years of not calling?"

"Son, I stopped calling because that's what your mom wanted. She wanted a clean slate and a life that didn't include me because she hated me for the mess that I got us into. She hated me because we lost you."

"Clearly she didn't care too much about losing me if she never came back." I finish off my beer.

"I know it doesn't mean much, but I'm here now. I'd like to start over. Get to know you."

"Do you have a job?" I ask.

"At a marina down the street. I've been picking up every shift that I can so I can rent a place and get out of that motel."

The server brings us another round and I consider his offer. Is he being genuine? It would be nice to have a parent of my own again.

Chapter 28

SLOANE · DECEMBER 2018

Ethan hasn't returned any of my calls or texts since Thanksgiving. Which, despite his lack of communication skills, is very unusual for him.

"Are you cooking?" I yell from the entryway. I can smell the scent of fresh basil and a new candle.

"Homemade pizzas!" Lauren screams back.

"Four?" I ask as I enter the kitchen. "Who's eating all of these?"

"I figured Miles and Ethan. One for each of us! We can do our own toppings."

"Oh, um," I stutter. I wrack my brain to figure out what kind of excuse to come up with for Ethan. I don't want to tell her the truth— that he's been ghosting me. "He's tied up at work, so we won't need one for him."

"More for us!" Lauren shrugs. A weight is lifted from my shoulders knowing that she doesn't suspect anything. I hate hiding things from Lauren, but I know what she'll say. She'll say exactly what I'm thinking.

He's pulling away again. This time though, I'm

completely aware.

After dinner, I do the dishes for Lauren and then escape to my room. I sit on the edge of my bed and stare at the lock screen on my phone. Six days. It's been almost a week of being left on delivered, not even on read. Which is even more frustrating considering I know he's read it. I hate how he has so much control over me. He knows my daily routine, when I leave for work and when I get home, so I know he's been leaving early and staying late to avoid running into me.

I launch my phone across the bed, and it falls into the sliver of space between the mattress and the wall. Silent tears fall down my face and soak the pillow that Ethan usually sleeps on. Why did I have to fall in love with someone that couldn't love me back? In the beginning, I was convinced he was my 'right person, wrong time'. Now, I'm starting to think that may just be a phrase people use when they love someone so deeply and know that person doesn't, and never can, love them back the same way. So instead, they'll make up excuses about timing and places to avoid the inevitable ending.

Knock. Knock.

Before I have the chance to wipe away my tears, Lauren is standing in the doorway.

"What's wrong?" I can hear the concern in her voice.

"Nothing, I'm fine. It's nothing." I sniffle.

"Clearly it's something."

"Ethan's been ignoring me for almost a week now."

"A week? Why didn't you say something sooner?"

"Because I'm embarrassed. It's happening again— I'm losing him, and I have absolutely no control over it. How am I back here? Why didn't I learn? I've been so convinced that the reason I never fully moved on was that we were supposed to try again. We were supposed to work out this time. So why haven't we? This might sound insane, and I don't even know if I believe in God, but sometimes I think that he wouldn't keep putting Ethan back into my life if we weren't meant to work out one day."

"Oh, Sloane." Lauren rubs my shoulder. "Or he's trying to teach you a lesson. You're not going to want to hear this, but you need to let him go. Look at what he's been doing to you for the past two years. You can't keep living like this, at his every beck and call. This is your life; he doesn't call the shots. You do."

I can't manage a reply. After a few minutes of silence and more sobbing, Lauren turns off the lamp on my nightstand and leaves the room. I fall asleep on top of my comforter, fully dressed in dried tears on both cheeks.

The next morning, I get in the shower and turn the water as hot as it will go in hopes that I can burn off any trace of Ethan. I dry myself off and stare at my naked body in the mirror, thinking about all the times he touched me. Why can't I remember the last time that he kissed me? What if the last time was the last time? I make myself sick over the thought and kneel in front of the toilet bowl.

I finish up in the bathroom and retrieve my phone from underneath my bed, where I left it last night. I power it on, grab my work bag and head out the door. As I get out of the elevator, I stare at the only text message I received.

Ethan Brady: Hey. I'm sorry for not replying. I needed some space.

That's it? That's all he has to say? I really hate him sometimes. I shove the phone back into my bag and, for once, read the advertisements plastered all over the subway car.

~

"You can't just ignore me for a week and expect me to forget about it, Ethan," I say, half angry and half annoyed. I slam the dishwasher shut and stare directly into his eyes.

"I know and I said I'm sorry," he replies, avoiding eye contact by looking down at his shoes. "What more do you want from me?"

"I want you to stop avoiding me. Stop avoiding us."

"I'm not. I needed to be alone."

"You can communicate that then, before ghosting me."

"I didn't ghost you, Sloane. I'm here now, aren't I?"

"Yeah, but for how long?" I sit on the barstool as Ethan paces the kitchen. Watching him walk back and forth, I wonder what he's thinking. I'd like to think that all my problems would be solved if I could just read his mind.

"I don't know," he replies. "If I could answer that, we'd be dating."

I stare blankly at him and feel a tear roll down my cheek. Two years ago, any time I'd been around Ethan, I was worried I would say the wrong thing and scare him away. Now, in the middle of our tiny New York City apartment, I'm being the most vulnerable I've ever been with anyone.

"I didn't mean that in a bad way." He sits on the stool next to me and puts his hand on my leg. "I just don't know what I can say that can make you understand how I'm feeling."

"I can't keep doing this one foot in one foot out thing

with you anymore. We're not in college anymore, Ethan. I want a relationship. No more of whatever this is." I sniffle and wipe away a tear before it hits my lip.

He ignores me for a moment and puts his head in his hands. This is it— this is the moment it all ends. I brace myself for his delivery. I know that's what he's thinking.

How do I tell her I can't give her what she wants?

"I've told you this before, Sloane. I need to do this at my own pace and on my own time."

I nod and ingest every word he's saying to me as if I haven't heard them hundreds of times before.

"Can you promise me something?" I ask.

"Depends." I watch him swallow.

"Please just don't leave me in the dark like that again. I want to be here for you. I'm on your side, but I can't do that if you ignore me for weeks on end."

"It was less than a week," he replies.

"I'm serious. It hurts."

"I'll try."

Ethan never makes promises he can't keep, which is why he doesn't make promises.

I empty the dishwasher and pour myself another glass of wine, knowing he's probably rolling his eyes behind my back. He plops himself onto the couch and plays on his phone. Is this what our life would be like— that future I've been dreaming of— would it be bad communication, half-assed promises and awkward silences? I'd like to think our relationship would be different once he's ready to put in the effort and fully commit.

"Should we watch *Breaking Bad*? I can pour you a glass." I hold up the wine bottle.

"I'm not in the mood to drink tonight," he says as he

turns on the episode we left off at.

Ethan's body molds to mine as we lay on the couch. I drink my wine too quickly and refill the glass three more times during the two episodes we get through. No matter how much I try, I can't get our last conversation out of my head. One of his arms is wrapped around my waist, while my head rests on the other.

"Let's go to bed." His mouth finds its way to my ear.

I turn around so that I'm facing him, even though his head is still a few inches above mine. My hand grips the back of his neck, I pull him into me, and we start kissing. Our mouths become one for what feels like hours. I can't remember the last time we kissed for this long. Maybe the first time we ever kissed? In the hallway the led to my bedroom in Ascent. I remember the first time we kissed like it happened hours ago. Sometimes I wish I didn't.

"My room?"

"I want to fuck you here," he whispers. "On the couch."

So, I let him. I let him fuck me on the sectional couch we got from Facebook Marketplace and the entire time I try not to cry. Somehow, it feels different than all the other times we've had sex. It feels less intimate, like I'm just an object to him. I try not to let it show, but something tells me he knows. Once we're done, we both lay there. Naked and completely still. Even though he was just inside of me, he feels so distant. How can I miss him when he's right here?

"Is it okay if I sleep at home tonight?" he asks, as if my opinion holds any weight.

"Okay," is all I can manage.

He gets dressed, washes out my wine glass and puts

his shoes on all while I lay naked on the couch. He kisses my forehead and leaves the apartment. I expect myself to cry, but I don't. I get off the couch and make my way into my room where I change into my favorite pajamas and get into bed. Even though it feels like something between us is about to break, something within me feels somewhat at peace.

I don't want to spend the rest of my life thinking "Is this my great love story?" because I want more. I deserve more. I don't want calls that go unanswered or texts that are never read. I don't want to spend holidays, or any day, begging someone to choose me. I deserve someone who chooses me without question. Someone who loves me without doubt. I want someone who shows up and I realize that my relationship with Ethan isn't any of those things. It likely never will be.

Maybe this really is the end.

Chapter 29

SLOANE · DECEMBER 2018

Phillip hands me a blush-colored envelope. My name is written in calligraphy and without even opening it, I know it's Graham and Emily's wedding invitation. The wedding isn't until summer but being early is on brand for them.

I enter our apartment that's filled with half-packed moving boxes and avoid opening the envelope. I place it on the counter and pull a bottle of white wine from the fridge. I pour a glass and stare at the envelope that sits in front of me.

Am I ready to open it?

I carefully open the envelope and immediately tear up. This is all I want— someone that loves me enough to commit to forever. Even though I know that marriage doesn't always mean forever, people don't go into it thinking they'll get divorced. They go into wanting to spend the rest of their lives together. Why can't Ethan give this to me?

I grab a magnet from the drawer next to the sink and

hang the invitation on the side of the refrigerator. My phone starts buzzing on the counter. I pick myself up off the floor and see a message from Ethan. I forgot we have plans tonight.

Ethan Brady: Waiting for our food now. Be there in about 20.

Even though most of our kitchen is packed, we left out a few wine glasses knowing we'd need them. I reach into the cabinet above the sink for one, pour myself a heavy glass of Cab and finish it before he arrives. Something tells me I'm going to need it.

"Did we both get the same thing?" he says, looking at the open to-go containers on the counter.

"Buffalo chicken wrap?" I ask.

He nods and reaches for two of the ketchup packages and squirts them on his fries. We eat in silence as the TV plays sports coverage from the living room. I scroll Instagram on my phone before pouring myself another glass of wine.

"What should we watch? We need a new show, but I haven't heard of anything good on Netflix."

"I can't do this anymore, Sloane." He cuts me off mid-sentence. "I think this, us, needs to end."

The wine glass in my hand falls to the floor and I immediately bend down to pick up the pieces. Tears fill my eyes as I pick up each piece and place it in my other hand. Here I am again, crying on our kitchen floor.

"Fuck!" Ethan shouts as he bends down next to me.

I look at my hand and notice there's a large piece of glass wedged into my palm. Why can't I feel it? I can see the glass and the blood, but I can't feel anything. The blood drips down my hand and onto the kitchen rug. I hope Lauren wasn't planning on taking this with her. Ethan pulls out his phone and helps me up. I watch as he calls an Uber and grabs my hand to inspect it.

"We should leave it in there. I'm worried about pulling it out. I don't want it to bleed more." He grabs a dish towel that's folded over the oven handle and wraps my hand in it. I'm still frozen in shock.

"Sloane, I'm so sorry," he says as he opens the car door. I get into the backseat, and he slides in next to me.

We arrive at the emergency room in what feels like seconds. I still can't manage to form words, so I can't tell him that I want him to leave. He checks us in and sits next to me in the waiting room, holding the dishtowel over my hand and applying the slightest pressure around where the glass is to stop the bleeding.

"Sloane Hart?" A doctor emerges.

We follow her through a door, and she shows me to a bed where I sit while she draws the curtain. I don't make eye contact with her or Ethan because if I do, I think I might be sick.

"This doesn't look too bad. I'm going to remove it and then clean the wound before wrapping it up. The cleaning will be the worst part."

I nod in place of a reply.

I feel no pain as she gets the glass out and cleans my hand. I'm trying to wrap my head around what Ethan said after dinner. He's had so many chances to end it. I've given him so many outs. And he chooses tonight?

The car ride home is silent. Even the driver isn't listening to music. All that I hear repeatedly in my head is, "I can't do this anymore Sloane". I hate how he says my name. I hope I never hear him say it again. We arrive at our building, and both stand outside for a moment before walking in.

"Should I come to yours so we can finish talking?" he asks.

"No. I don't think we need to talk," I reply, still avoiding eye contact.

I finally look up and stare at him. I always believed that we would find our way back to each other every time, but this time it feels final, like I'll never see him again. Or if I do, it'll be different. I know it in my bones; this is it.

"I just need you to know that you can't do this to me anymore. There's no going back after tonight. I can't keep doing this to myself anymore. I love you so much that it hurts. It's made me physically ill on more than one occasion. Love shouldn't hurt. Love shouldn't make you sick. I know that you're not ready and nothing I can say or do will ever change that. The only person that can change that is you. I would've done anything for you—" A tear falls down my face.

I wait for him to say something, but he doesn't. We look at each other for a few seconds and then I break eye contact, turn around and walk into the building. I never look back.

The elevator ride feels centuries long. As soon as I'm face to face with the empty apartment, I break down. Everything is just as we left it. Our empty take-out boxes waiting to be brought to the trash chute, the remnants of my broken wine glass, blood-stained paper towels. I do my best to clean it up without hurting myself again.

I always believed that we'd find our way back to each

other every time things ended. Except this time, it feels final— like I'd never see him again. Even though I know that's not true since we still live in the same building. I can feel it in my bones. This time is really it.

It still hurts. Losing him and missing him still hurts, but in a different way than it did the other times. It doesn't feel like an earth-shattering heartbreak, but a more subtle lingering pain. I stay up most of the night replaying our relationship over in my head from the moment we met all the way up to tonight. Our first kiss, our first date, our last kiss and our last date. I wish things could have unfolded differently between us. I know that deep down he loves and cares about me, but it still isn't enough.

Some people don't grow up in a house full of love, and even though my parents aren't together anymore, for 18 years of my life they had a good run. I hate what I know about Ethan's past, and I wish he felt like he could tell me. In more ways than one I hate his parents. I hate them for leaving him, but I hate them even more for making him feel like he isn't deserving of being loved.

Chapter 30

ETHAN · DECEMBER 2018

When I got back into the city, I avoided replying to Sloane's texts. It's now been two more days and I don't know what to say to make this any better. Even though she won't admit it, I know she's upset with me for ditching her on Thanksgiving. So, I can't imagine how she feels now that I've been M.I.A. for a few days. Why do I do this to myself? Why do I do this to her? I wish I knew. I wish I was easy to understand. I wish I could understand my own thoughts and actions. Yet here we are.

I throw the laundry bag over my shoulder and head into the elevator when I decide to finally text her back. I give no explanation to where I've been. Instead I just apologize, knowing she'll interrogate me in person later.

I walk into her apartment and notice that there's a half empty bottle of wine on the counter. Part of me was expecting that— she always drinks when she's nervous. Usually, I don't mind it, but for some reason, today it really bothers me. It makes me wonder if alcohol is a coping mechanism for her. I can't build a life with someone who turns to alcohol when things get tough. Alcohol is the sole reason my life ended up the way that it did. I'll never forgive either of my parents for choosing alcohol over me.

"I want you to stop avoiding me. Stop avoiding us," she addresses me.

"I'm not. I just needed space," I answer.

"You can communicate that then, before ghosting me."

"I didn't ghost you. I'm here now, aren't I?"

"Yeah, but for how long?"

"I don't know," I reply. "If I could answer that, we'd be dating."

She stares at me, and I can see the heartbreak in her eyes. I need to choose my words more carefully because you'd think I ended things with her by the way she just broke in front of me. She didn't even have to say or do anything. I notice the change in her demeanor almost immediately.

"Sloane, I didn't mean that in a bad way." I sit next to her. "I just don't know what I can say that can make you understand how I'm feeling."

"I can't keep doing this one foot in one foot out thing with you anymore. We're not in college anymore, Ethan. I want a relationship. No more of whatever this is."

God, I wish I could just tell her everything.

"I'll try." I regret those two words as soon as they leave my mouth. I know I'll never be the person she wants or deserves. I need to just let her go and stop trying to be someone I'm not.

~

I spend the next few days thinking through everything. Every moment in my childhood, every moment before

218

Sloane and every moment with Sloane. I tried to remember the last time I was truly happy, and it hurt to know that I couldn't pinpoint it. Couldn't most people? My entire life has been a series of unfortunate events. One after another. How shitty is that? What's even shittier though is having to explain these things to people— people like Sloane.

It's not that I don't want to tell her, I just can't. I don't know how. I don't want to see that look of pity in her eyes. I don't want anyone to pity me but especially not her. I'm supposed to be the one she leans on, not the opposite way around. I'll never depend on someone in the way she wants me to. I'll never depend on someone other than myself because often, people let me down. They always have and they always will.

I stand in line waiting to pay for our dinner and can't shake the sinking feeling inside of me. I know I need to do this.

"Order for Ethan?" The host hands me a plastic bag with two to-go boxes inside in exchange for my credit card.

The restaurant is six blocks away from our apartment building which gives me time to run through how I want this to go down. I hate that I'm going to hurt her, which is why I've put this off for so long. I prepare the conversation in my head and go over it what feels like a hundred times.

The elevator doors open and a lump in my throat starts to form. I don't want to do this, I really don't, but at the same time I know I have no choice. Nothing between us will change if I can't get my shit together first. I just hope she understands that.

I let myself into Sloane's apartment and greet her with a hug.

"Thank you for picking dinner up! I'm starving." She opens the bag and each container when I realize we both ordered the same thing. Buffalo chicken wraps.

It reminds me of the time we went to Jerry's with Graham and Lauren after the volleyball tournament. I didn't know it at the time, but looking back, that day was the first time I realized that my feelings for Sloane were more than just sexual.

"What should we watch tonight?" Sloane asks.
I take a bite out of my wrap and chew extra slowly so I can delay responding to her for as long as possible.

"We need a new show, but I haven't heard of anything good on Netflix." I cut her off before she can finish.

"I can't do this anymore, Sloane. I think this, us, needs to end."

I watch the color drain from her face as she drops the wine glass that she was just about to take a sip from. She immediately bends down to clean it up, as if it's instinct, and that's when I notice the blood. This is going so much worse than I ever expected.

The hospital visit is short, but it feels so long. Probably because I'm still avoiding the conversation that we inevitably still need to have. The car ride home is painfully silent, and I try to put myself into her shoes. I wonder what she's thinking and how she's feeling. Does she hate me? Is it selfish to wonder that? The driver pulls up to our building and I watch as Sloane pauses for a second before opening the car door. Within seconds, we're face to face with each other in the middle of the sidewalk.

"We don't need to talk, Ethan. This is it."

I don't bother arguing with her because I know she's right. She deserves someone better than me. Someone who can give her everything I'll never be capable of. Feeling deflated, I watch as she turns and walks into the lobby. I expect her to look back, but she never does. I don't know if I ever pictured things with Sloane actually ending, but this feels final. I hate that I'm hurting her, but even more so, I hate that I can't be honest with her. I hope she knows that there wasn't anything she could've done differently.

The cold air feels comforting as I wait a few minutes until I know she's gotten inside of her apartment to make my way upstairs. My roommates are sitting on the couch smoking weed and watching college basketball, so I join them.

"Want a hit?" Noah holds out the bong.

I grab the bong from him without replying and rip it one, two, three times.

"Woah dude, bad day?" Lucas asks.

"You could say that," I reply.

None of us speak for the rest of the night. Instead, we get high, avoid our problems and watch sports. Three of the things that I do best.

~

I roll over in bed and reach for my phone to scroll Instagram. It's not until I see a post that I want to send to Sloane that I remember everything that unfolded last night. I miss her more than I thought I would. I know because I feel a little more empty than usual.

What's wrong with me? Why am I so fucked up? I mean, I know why I'm fucked up— my parents did this to me. Why can't I let someone love me when it's all I've wanted my entire life? All I've wanted was to feel loved and as soon as someone tries, I push them away.

I really thought if I let Sloane love me, eventually I'd get there with her too. Instead, here we are. Three breakups, two years, and one really broken heart.

Chapter 31

SLOANE · DECEMBER 2018

Today I decide to walk home from work because I can't imagine dealing with an overcrowded subway car right now. The air is crisp and unusually warm for mid-December. I still zip my coat all the way up to my chin to avoid getting sick. The last thing I need is to miss more time at work. I ruminate on the last three, almost four, years as I walk down Park Ave. I pull my headphones out of my pocket, plug them into my phone and scroll Spotify to find a solid break up playlist, filled with just the right amount of Taylor Swift.

I'm reminded of the night when I tried to convince Ethan that we should walk almost seven miles home because I would've done anything for more time with him. It's funny how some things never change. Now here I am years later, in a different city, wishing the same thing.

I walk into the apartment and am greeted by Lauren, who already has a drink waiting for me.

"Get ready," she demands. "We're going out."

I smile as I enter my room, observing the few pieces of clothing that I haven't packed yet. I pull my favorite bodysuit off its hanger along with the jeans that used to fit me perfectly, but now gapes a little in the back, and get dressed. I sit at my vanity to reapply mascara and lip gloss. Lauren emerges behind a stack of boxes and sets a margarita in front of me.

"Do you want to talk about it?" I watch her through the mirror as she sits on my bed.

"Not really, there's nothing to talk about."

"How are you feeling?" she asks.

"Oddly enough, I'm kind of okay," I admit. "I saw it coming. I think I just tried not to."

We throw on coats and Lauren calls us an Uber to Miles' place so she can drop off a few of her boxes on the way to the new bar in Chelsea that she's taking me to. His loft is a New York City dream. It's everything I used to picture we'd live in until I realized most people can't afford it. Exposed brick, high ceilings and a spiral staircase that takes you up to the lofted bedroom and full bath.

"This is amazing." I gawk.

"Isn't it?" She drops the boxes near the front door.

"Where's Miles?" I ask.

"Out with clients. Want a drink before we go?" She nods towards a glass cabinet full of liquor. "The rooftop is amazing. We can go sit up there if it's not too cold."

"Sure."

I make my way around the loft admiring every detail, hoping I'll live like this one day. I follow her down the hall to the elevator and we take it up two floors. The doors open to an empty hallway with one door at the end of it. I follow her through it and watch as a gorgeous view of the city emerges.

"Wow," I breathe.

She leads me to two sling chairs and we both take a seat, wrapping blankets around us even though we're in winter coats. We sit silently as I look across the landscape of what is essentially the best view in the city. Or at least, the best view I've had. From up here, the city seems so large, yet so small. I can see people partying on other rooftops, couples making dinner through their windows, cars zipping through traffic below.

"Are you going to be okay?" Lauren breaks the silence. I turn to her because I'm unsure if she's joking or not, but the concern in her eyes tells me she's serious. She's worried about me.

"Lauren." I put my hand on hers. "I'll be fine."

"I just feel shitty," she admits. "Like of course this happens as I'm moving out. Timing's a bitch."

"It always is." I laugh.

We never end up going out. Instead, Lauren brings up a bottle of tequila, a space heater and an extension cord as we run through the entirety of our friendship.

"I think my favorite memory of you, a story we'll definitely tell our kids when they're heading off to college, is junior year spring break," Lauren says.

"Which part?" I pass the bottle back to her.

"When you almost got arrested at that bar in Key West. I'll never forget the look on your face when the bouncer snatched your ID and told you to stand to the side. I've literally never seen you run, ever, except for that day," she snorts.

"I can't believe he didn't recognize us when we went

back an hour later. All we did was swap sunglasses and t-shirts."

"Wait, remember sophomore year when we were so excited to use our new fake IDs and then the bouncer at Jerry's peeled the film off of them and told us to get lost?" She cackles.

"That was easily one of the top five most embarrassing moments in my life. Everyone behind us in line looked at us like we were idiots."

"We were idiots." She takes a swig of tequila and makes a face.

"I can't believe we're taking a bottle of liquor to the face right now."

"Can you not? We used to do this every weekend with Burnetts and Bacardi."

"Oh God, don't remind me." I pretend to gag.

We laugh so hard I almost pee my pants and then recount more of our favorite stories. The day we met at our dorm hall orientation, the first time we got drunk together, senior year spending hours applying to any job we could find, thinking we'd never land one in a city like this. Yet here we are. Sitting on the rooftop of the apartment she now shares with what I'd like to consider her soulmate. I'm so proud of her but a little sad for me.

I look at the time on my phone. It's nearing midnight which is late for a Wednesday. I call an Uber and Lauren walks me outside.

"Hey, Sloane?" she says, grabbing my shoulder.

"Yeah?"

"One day he's going to wake up and realize that he lost the best thing he ever had. He lost the only person who would've loved him through anything. I hope he hurts. I hope he regrets. But even more importantly, I hope he learns. I hope he learns that love isn't always easy. Love is compromise. Love is understanding. Love is accepting. Someone else is going to give you all of that and more one day, and I can't wait to see who he is."

"I love you." I hug her and get into the car.

A few minutes into the ride, a wave of nausea hits me. I'm more drunk than I thought. I wonder if it's from the lack of sleep or the lack of food. Either way I try to close my eyes and stay off my phone to keep me from getting sick and being charged a cleaning fee. The ride takes unusually long, so I open my eyes and notice we're taking a longer way through the West Village. Before I can close them again, I see Reese's building. Out of nowhere, I start to cry.

In the backseat of what's probably turning into a $50 Uber ride, I'm crying because I broke up with a guy who loved me for a guy that never could. Why am I the way that I am? I scroll through my contacts until I see Reese Thompson. My finger wavers over the call button, but eventually I hold the phone up to my ear. It rings and rings. No answer. I lock the phone and close my eyes until we get to my apartment.

When I finally get into bed, I reach for the charger to plug my phone into. Before I set my alarm and go sleep, I pull up Instagram and type Reese's name into the search bar. I'm surprised to see he unblocked me.

There it is— a picture of him with what I'm assuming is his new girlfriend at a wedding a few weeks ago. The cliché caption "Forever wedding date." confirms it. I stare at the screen and debate my next move. Before I can stop myself, I hit send on a text to Ethan.

Me: Can you sleep here? Just for tonight? I don't want to be alone.

I put my phone on do not disturb even though I continue to check it every few minutes until he replies.

Ethan Brady: We both know that's a bad idea.

Staring at his message, I start crying all over again. Now I need to learn how to get used to a bed without him in it. It's cold, sad and lonely. I hate it.

I toss and turn all night, unable to turn off my brain. All I can think about is Ethan. What if I never get over him? What if I go to bed and wake up every day for the rest of my life wanting him? What if I keep waiting for a call or a text or a sign that never comes? What if he's the one but I'm not?

Epilogue

SLOANE · JUNE 2019

It's been six months since Ethan ended things between us. I haven't seen or heard from him, not even a happy birthday text. I think back to who I was in December— it seems like such a long-lost version of myself, someone I don't know anymore. Losing Ethan made me realize that I didn't mourn the memories of him. I mourned the idea of him that I created. I mourned the future I built in my head using our best moments. I mourned the potential I saw in him, and the life that I saw for us.

I make my way into the kitchen of my studio apartment in the West Village and watch as my cat, Ollie, perches himself on the windowsill above the sink. I never thought of myself as a cat person, but a dog seems like too much for the city. I turn on the coffee pot and reach for a muffin in the pastry case my mom brought me when she helped me move in. Once it's brewed, I pour myself a cup and sit at the bistro table where I begin each morning.

Right after the breakup, if you could even call it that, I turned back to writing in my journal. I wrote in it every day, multiple times a day, and have filled two so far. Annie gave me the idea of starting a blog so that all my professional work didn't revolve around love. I loved the idea so much that I worked on it all night. In just three months, I had gained over 25,000 subscribers. Now, each morning I wake up and write for an hour before I head into the office. As I sip my coffee, I stare at the blank screen that sits in front of me as I try and figure out today's post.

The most important thing that I've learned over the last six months is that it's so important to show up for yourself. Spend time getting to know who you are, find new hobbies, fall back in love with old ones. For me, reading and therapy have helped a lot. Both have been a reminder of how beautiful, sometimes sad but mostly beautiful, life is.

"There is so much more to life than finding someone who will want you or being sad over someone who doesn't," is a quote from Emery Allen that I keep finding myself referring back to, especially on those harder days. It's a great reminder that our time here is limited, why waste it on someone who doesn't want you around?

I read the words on the screen and try to convince myself that I believe them. Sure, I'm proud of myself for how far I've come in six months, but it hasn't been easy and there are days I still cry because I miss him. I remember when I thought I couldn't live without him. I remember when I thought I'd never meet anyone like him when, really, he was just another person who was coming and going from my life. He's someone who taught me things that I could never teach myself. He taught me how to fall in love. He taught me how to be vulnerable, with myself and others. He taught me that I'm too sure of myself to be crying over someone who isn't ready for me. He taught me how to love myself the way he never could.

~

Lauren and I have plans to grab coffee before I'm due at work. I quickly get dressed and head to Ralph's, our new favorite spot to meet.

"Hey, babe! Got you a vanilla latte already."

"You didn't have to grab mine but thank you!" I hug her. "How are you? Was this a hike from Chelsea?"

"Not really, I mean, yes, but I never come into midtown, so I don't mind. Plus, I don't have to get the boys until noon today, so I had nothing else going on."

"How's living together?" I stir the straw in my iced latte out of nervous habit.

"Good!" Her face lights up. "How are you? All packed and ready for the wedding?"

"Eh." I stir the straw faster. "I'm not sure."

"Why? What's making you the most anxious? Seeing Ethan or spending a weekend away with Blake?"

"I guess a little bit of both. It's been six months but…"

"Sloane, it's been six months. You've gotten through six months without him, that's great! Stop looking at it the opposite way around. Go to the wedding with Blake and just have fun. Remember? That was the whole point of keeping things going with him— to have fun. So, do that okay? Have fun, get drunk, dance a little, and try not to pay any attention to Ethan."

"You're right, you're right." I laugh.

I met Blake through a co-worker just over a month ago. We went on one date and have basically just been hooking up since then. We have chemistry but I'm not sure it's romantic at all with him. He's great to look at and have sex with though— piercing blue eyes, brownish-blonde hair, and abs that make me never want to eat again. Blake is my meantime guy. He's good for now but not forever.

"So, what really is it?" she asks again.

"I'm just scared. We're getting older and life is changing. People are moving in together, getting engaged, getting married and then there's me."

"And then there's you?" She practically chokes on her coffee. "Sloane, look at everything you've done. You have your dream job; you can afford to live alone in the West Village, and you started a blog that's basically like an older sister to girls going through the same things you've experienced. You can't worry about other people's timelines, none of us can, because they'll always be different. Just keep doing what you're doing, and things will fall into place. They always have."

"You're the best. You know that right?"

"I mean, duh."

~

Blake has been coming over about once a week, but I've never let him sleep here. I tried to make a no-sleepover rule after Ethan. Sleepovers make things messy and when things are messy, I get attached. Tonight though, he's spending the night because we have an early morning flight to catch. Since we'll already be spending a weekend away together, breaking the rule tonight won't kill me.

I'm still extremely anxious about this entire situation. I didn't necessarily want to bring him to the wedding but after two months of this being the main topic of discussion in therapy, my therapist decided that I need a distraction at the wedding, preferably one that I can flirt with. Which is exactly why I'm bringing Blake instead of Lauren. It also doesn't hurt that he's hot and might make Ethan a little jealous. That is, if he's there alone anyway.

~

I wake up to a shirtless Blake and admire his abs before snapping back to reality. Maybe I could get used to this? I try to erase the thought from my mind as I quietly get out of bed to get ready for the airport. After a few minutes in the bathroom, he comes in without knocking and opens the toilet seat while I'm mid-makeup routine.

"I can leave," I offer, scrambling to find my phone.

"Oh, it's okay, it's just a piss."

I shudder at his reply and walk into the kitchen until he's done. A few seconds later he walks out in just his boxers and plops himself onto my couch. Even though he's great to look at, his presence is still slightly annoying. Excusing myself, I go back into the bathroom to finish my makeup and put on the outfit I laid out last night.

"We need to leave in probably 15 minutes," I say to Blake who's scrolling on his phone.

"Sure thing, I can be ready in 10." He practically jumps off the couch and heads for the bedroom.

While I'm waiting for him, I zip my carry-on suitcase up and set it near the front door next to his duffle. I look over the note I'm leaving for Lauren one last time to make sure all of Ollie's instructions make sense. Lauren isn't exactly a cat person, so I was reluctant to ask her to check in on him, but she insisted— as she always does.

"Ready?" Blake comes up behind me and grabs my hips.

"I just need to call us an Uber."

He kisses my neck as my fingers move quickly across my phone screen to find us the first available driver.

I appreciate that he's trying to be comforting. Half of my anxiety surrounding this trip is the fact that I'll be traveling and spending a weekend with someone who isn't my boyfriend. He isn't Ethan. He isn't Reese. He's Blake. A guy I've been fucking for one month. I barely even know him and I'm about to spend a weekend with him? Not just any weekend, *the* weekend— the first time I'll be in the same room as Ethan since our "breakup", not to mention the first time I'll be on a flight with a guy. I'm spiraling.

I take a deep breath and look down at my phone to see the notification that our driver is a minute out. Blake grabs both of our bags and heads toward the stairs as I follow slightly behind. Maybe this won't be such a bad weekend after all.

~

We arrive at the venue and there are already at least a hundred people seated in white wooden chairs. For a second, I think about how this could've been Lauren and Graham's wedding. I lead Blake to two seats towards the front that are still open, and he puts his hand on my thigh as soon as we sit down. Within minutes music starts playing and everyone goes quiet. The groomsmen start to descend the aisle and I watch one by one until I notice the back of his head. When he gets up to the altar, he stands to the right of the best man, Graham's brother, and I watch him scan the crowd. Is he looking for me? And just like that, he finds me.

A slight smile falls over his face and my entire body

locks up. My heart sinks to my stomach as I realize I'm in the crowd, watching him stand at an altar and it's not our wedding. It never will be. I used to dream about the day we'd eventually figure out our qualms— he'd ask me to be his girlfriend, we'd move in together after a year or so, and soon after he'd propose to me in Central Park or on a rooftop when I least expected it. I thought about what it would be like to have the guy who wasn't sure about love or commitment finally get down on one knee because he knew I was the one he wanted to spend the rest of his life with. But this moment isn't that.

Instead, we both exist in the same room and act as though we're strangers now. A polite smile is the only moment we share. No small talk or asking how each other has been because it hurts too much to know. It hurts too much to go back there again. I know he feels it too.

Countless nights I've tossed and turned, wondering if the end of us affected him as much as it did me. Or even slightly. I watch his eyes glance over to Blake, back to me, and to Blake once again. Immediately he looks down at his feet and I know exactly what he's feeling. The same pain I've felt almost every night since we parted ways on that sidewalk in Murray Hill. The pain of wanting something you can never have. The pain of wondering if it was the right person at the wrong time or just the wrong person. The pain of his first real heartbreak.

I often wondered if he ever loved me because he was never able to say it. Sometimes I felt it though— in quiet car rides, in the way his heart would beat faster whenever my head rested on his chest, in the smaller moments that I can hardly remember now. I know he loved me, and I'd like to think that a part of him still does. Maybe, like me, a part of him always will.

The pianist strikes the keys to the tune of "Can't Help Falling in Love" by Elvis Presley and the guests rise to their feet to watch the bride's grand entrance. With a trembling hand, I intertwine my fingers with Blake's, and he reassures me with a gentle squeeze. The entire room is left in awe as Emily glides gracefully down the aisle. She's beautiful. I turn around to look at Ethan and our eyes lock in an unbreakable connection. I wonder if he's thinking the same thing I am. *I wish this could be us.*

"We're gathered here today to witness the union of Emily Miller and Graham Clark. Marriage is a journey that will have its ups and downs. It's not always easy, but it's worth it. To make a marriage work, it takes love, patience, understanding and forgiveness. It's a bond that grows stronger each day."

"Graham, you've showed me nothing but unconditional love since the day I met you. Throughout our relationship, your love for me has never wavered. You've never made me question or doubt how important to you I am, because you show me every day," Emily says.

As I sit in the third row, taking in every word of their vows, tears stream down my face. It isn't that I'm not happy for Graham and Emily; in fact, I'm elated to see them so in love. But as I listen to her speak about unconditional love, I can't help but think about the way I loved Ethan. I had been the only person in his life that wanted to love him through anything. Even after years of being strung along, confused and hurt I still loved him through it.

Here's the thing about unconditional love though— it

isn't one sided. It isn't standing in someone's doorway begging to be let in. It isn't taking your heart out of your chest, bloody and beating, and handing it to someone to do whatever they want with it. Unconditional love is someone breaking down the cage of your ribs to get your heart and you trusting they'll protect it just the same.

This isn't one of those beautiful love stories where they get back together in the end. This is one of those stories where the hurt and the confusion consumes them. It's one of those stories where the person who is in pain gets up, brushes themselves off and realizes their worth.

As much as I've always wanted to end up with Ethan, I think I knew he'd never be it for me. Is it scary to think about falling in love again? Opening my heart up to someone who could potentially damage it even worse than he did? Of course, it is. But that's what love is right? Love is taking risks regardless of the outcome.

Our relationship may not have been conventional. It wasn't a fairytale romance that we'd tell our kids and grandkids about one day. It was comfortable silences, familiar laughs and hugs that felt like home. What we had wasn't something I could ever put into words. It was just us.

Call it what you want, but for me, it was love.

Acknowledgements

Younger me, there are so many things I wish that I could tell you. I'm sorry you spent so many years alone with feelings of doubt, wondering if you were too much or maybe not enough. All those experiences brought us this book. So many people are or have been exactly where you were once and now, you're giving them something no author ever gave you— a story that makes them feel less alone and more understood. I'm so proud of you.

Natalie, Mom and Dad, you've always supported anything I've wanted to try, never doubted me and always cheered me on. You'll always be my favorite faces to see in any crowd. Mom, thanks for giving me your love of reading and your thoughtful, yet honest, criticism. Dad, thanks for giving me your drive, without it I would've never finished this book. Natalie, your creativity inspires me every day. I can't wait to see what the future of film holds for you.

Michaela, in ways this book wrote itself every time I picked up the phone to call you. Your honesty, kind heart and belly laughs got me through my first heartbreak and your endless support made this book go from a small idea to a big reality. I'll never be able to explain what that means.

Meg, you reminded me that good things take time and in pockets of doubt assured me that I could do it. I always knew you would be one of the first people to read it. Hailey, there was never a doubt in my mind that you would design the cover of this book and it turned into something that I can't even put into words. You captured the beauty of this story perfectly. Kim, your edits helped round out the final story. Thank you for always pushing me to my full potential and challenging me when I need it the most.

Grandma and Poppy, when I think of reading and writing, you're the first two faces that come to mind. From listening to me make up stories since the day I could talk, to Barnes and Noble visits, to reading side by side on the beach in Marco Island— this book kind of started with you.

To my family and friends, you know who you are, thank you for being just that. Each of you have shaped so many parts within this story and I'm eternally grateful.

Reading Group Guide

1. From the moment Sloane laid eyes on Ethan, she was hooked. Why do you think she was drawn to him before they had met? Have you ever felt that way about someone?

2. Why do you think Ethan's chapters were structured much shorter and vaguer than Sloane's?

3. Put yourself in Lauren's shoes, have you ever had a friend in a toxic on-and-off relationship? Focusing on Sloane's perspective only, did this novel help you understand why it can be hard for that friend to let go? If so, how?

4. Discuss the role Graham played in Sloane's life. Do you think he was right to share Ethan's personal experiences with Sloane behind his back?

5. Though on different scales, Sloane and Ethan both had traumatic events occur in their past. How did divorce and abandonment affect how they each gave and received love?

6. Do you think Ethan loved Sloane and was too emotionally immature to admit it? Or do you think he was leading her on? Explain why.

7. What was your favorite quote from the novel? Why did it stand out to you?

8. What does the title *Call It What You Want* mean to you after reading the book?

About the Author

Alissa DeRogatis is a writer based in Charlotte, North Carolina. *Call It What You Want* is her debut novel and is a love letter to all girls who have had a hard time getting over someone they never dated.

Always anxious, unfiltered, and on time, Alissa is a creative— a social media manager by day, and an up-and-coming author by night. She is an extrovert, a picky eater and an overthinker who always wants to incite deep conversation. She likes books, red wine, sad songs, and writing things she hopes you'll read. Follow her on all socials at @alissaderogatis.